Ticket to India

Also by N. H. Senzai

Shooting Kabul

Saving Kabul Corner

Ticket to India

N. H. Senzai

A Paula Wiseman Book
Simon & Schuster Books for Young Readers
NEW YORK LONDON TORONTO SYDNEY NEW DELHI

SIMON & SCHUSTER BOOKS FOR YOUNG READERS
An imprint of Simon & Schuster Children's Publishing Division
1230 Avenue of the Americas, New York, New York 10020

SIMON & SCHUSTER BOOKS FOR YOUNG READERS
is a trademark of Simon & Schuster, Inc.
For information about special discounts for bulk purchases, please contact
Simon & Schuster Special Sales at 1-866-506-1949 or business@simonandschuster.com.
The Simon & Schuster Speakers Bureau can bring authors to your live event. For
more information or to book an event, contact the Simon & Schuster Speakers
Bureau at 1-866-248-3049 or visit our website at www.simonspeakers.com.
Book design by Chloë Foglia
The text for this book is set in Bembo.
Manufactured in the United States of America
1015 FFG
2 4 6 8 10 9 7 5 3 1
Library of Congress Cataloging-in-Publication Data
Senzai, N. H.
Ticket to india / N.H. Senzai.—First edition.
pages cm
"A Paula Wiseman Book."
Summary: When twelve-year-old Maya and big sister Zara set off on their own
from Delhi to their grandmother's home of Aminpur, a small town in Northern
India, they become separated and Maya decides to continue their quest to find a chest
of family treasures that their grandmother's family left behind when they fled from
India to Pakistan during the Great Partition.
ISBN 978-1-4814-2258-1 (hardcover)
ISBN 978-1-4814-2260-4 (eBook)
[1. India—Fiction. 2. India—History--Partition, 1947—Fiction. 3. Adventure and
adventurers—Fiction. 4. Families—Fiction.] I. Title.
PZ7.S47953Ti 2015
[Fic]—dc23
2015013276

FIRST
EDITION

For *Naniamma* and *Dadiamma*—formidable grandmothers who withstood the tide of Partition with iron wills, intelligence, and grace.

And to all *Muhajirs*—émigrés who travel great distances to create new lives in an adopted homeland.

—N. H. S.

*There is a little bit of Indian in every Pakistani
and a little bit of Pakistani in every Indian.*

—BENAZIR BHUTTO (PRIME MINISTER OF PAKISTAN)

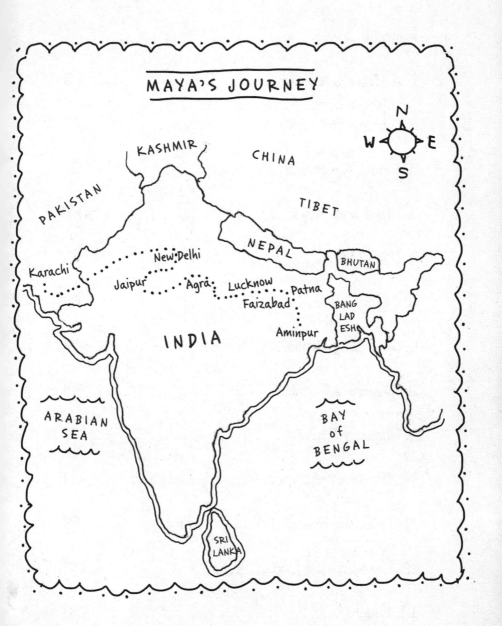

CONTENTS

Prologue

Wednesday, September 14
30,000 feet above the Pacific Ocean

When I was born, my parents had an epic argument at the hospital over my name. My mom wanted to name me after her father's mother. My dad wanted a name that would match my personality, which is bizarre considering he'd only known me for two days. But he swore that the moment he'd stared into my eyes, he'd remembered an old saying: "Still waters run deep." I had to look that up later, and found out that it's something you say about people who speak little but have interesting and complicated personalities. I don't know if that's a compliment or an insult, but my father insists it's a compliment.

The nurse finally made my parents fill out the birth certificate, so they had to compromise: My name is Maya Quddusiyyah Agha. I'm seriously glad that my dad got his choice in first. Don't get me wrong; both names have cool meanings. Quddusiyyah means "glorious," while Maya, also an old Arabic word, means "princess." Maya also translates into "eternal spring" in Hebrew, and "love" in Nepali. But can you imagine starting kindergarten and having to spell a name with eleven letters?

Later, it was my mom's youngest sister, who teaches English at the University of Arkansas, who told me about all the other Mayas who've come before me. I found out that most of them are pretty legendary: A Maya was the mother of the Greek god Hermes, and another gave birth to the founder of Buddhism. Maya is also another name for the Hindu goddess Durga, who is believed to be invincible as the power behind the creation, protection, and destruction of the world.

• • •

Maya stared down at the first entry of the journal she'd been assigned by Mrs. Hackworth and realized that she'd veered off course. *Too much personal information,* she thought, and sighed. But she couldn't help it—writing helped soothe her nerves and brought order to the chaotic thoughts jumbled inside her head. Her eraser hovered over the lines. But she *was* supposed to introduce herself, then write about *all* aspects of her trip, so she continued.

I'm on my way to Karachi, Pakistan, for the tenth time. I've gone every year since I was born, minus the two years when my dad changed jobs and when my older sister, Zara, broke her leg—she's always been a bit of a klutz. But here I am again, somewhere over the island of Fiji. Honestly, I would give anything not to be here. Because unlike with the other visits, Nanabba, my mother's father, won't be waiting at the airport to pick us up.

Maya's fingers stilled, clenching the pencil as a memory flooded her mind. At first it was a muddle of pastels, like staring at an unfocused impressionist painting. Soon angles and distinct forms came into focus in bold primary colors. It was nine months ago, a cool December day, and she was shimmying down the scratchy purple trunk of the peepal tree to join her grandfather in the rose garden. He handed her a set of pruning shears, and as the comfortable weight rested in her palm, he bent back a thorny branch.

"Did you know," he said, warm eyes twinkling, "when Alexander the Great invaded India over fifteen hundred years ago, he was amazed at the wealth of plants he encountered—roses in particular. So he sent clippings to his mentor, the great philosopher Aristotle."

Maya nodded, trying not to prick her finger as her mind wandered toward lunch, which the cook was preparing in the kitchen. Savory smells invaded the garden, which was surrounded by the high white walls that encircled villas in well-to-do neighborhoods.

The memory faded and Maya slumped in her airplane seat, eyes flooding with tears. She would never talk with her beloved *nanabba* again; he was dead, soon to be buried within the soil from which his beloved roses sprang.

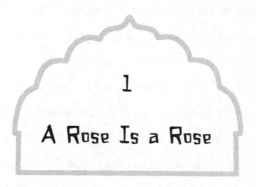

1

A Rose Is a Rose

THE MOMENT THEY ARRIVED, after an exhausting twenty-hour flight, they found the house, usually an oasis of calm, in chaos. Zara stumbled through the carved wooden doors first, while Maya entered last, sweaty from the soaring temperatures outside, a sharp contrast to cool, temperate San Francisco. She closed her eyes for a moment, watching a kaleidoscope of colors flash behind her eyelids—vibrant images that assaulted her senses each time she arrived. The sun seemed brighter here, more gold than yellow, raining heat down over the dusty city of Karachi. She opened her eyes and her pupils adjusted to the shadowy foyer, decorated in calming white, cream, and powder blue.

While her sister pushed past teary relatives to launch herself into her grandmother's arms with a dramatic sob, Maya stood back. She was stunned to see how her grandmother appeared to have aged a decade since she last saw her. Her usually meticulously wrapped sari was askew, and her silver hair, always pulled back in an elegant chignon, was wild around her shoulders. *Naniamma* had always been the strong, solid partner in her grandparents' marriage and Maya had never seen her cry, let alone fall apart like this. But as soon as *Naniamma* set eyes on Maya, she beckoned her for an enveloping hug. Before Maya could loosen her tongue and come up with something comforting to say, her mother gently pulled *Naniamma* away.

"*Ammi*," Dalia whispered, "I just can't believe *Abbu* is gone."

They clung to one another for a long minute, until a tight-lipped great-aunt guided them to the living room, with its ornate wooden sofas and embroidered cushions. As the adults and Zara huddled together, passing around a box of tissues, Maya stood, forgotten. Fighting the urge to hide under the dining room table as she had when she was a child, she spotted one of her grandfather's paintings hanging across from her, an abstract swirl of cool blues and beiges. She remembered the day he'd painted it, while on a picnic on Hawksbay beach. When he had been alive and healthy. Heart heavy, she slunk off with her backpack, up the stairs to the empty television lounge.

Longing to hear a comforting voice, she picked up the phone and dialed her home number in California. She wanted to tell her father that they'd reached Karachi safely. When the rings rolled over into voice mail, she realized he was probably out, dealing with burial plots, headstones, and other preparations for *Nanabba*'s funeral, which was to take place in San Francisco in a week. Restless, she went to the towering bookshelves that lined the room. She passed business, mathematics, poetry, and old novels, until she reached the section on history and politics. She pulled out a history book, titled *The Struggle for Pakistan*. On the way to the sofa, she switched on the television to a soap opera in Urdu. While her brain tried to adjust to a language she understood but didn't speak much, she glumly opened her backpack.

Sixth grade had started two weeks before, and Maya had been thrilled that her best friends, Olivia and Kavita, had been assigned to the same homeroom. But even before she could get used to a new class schedule, the news of her grandfather had come. And now, being away for more than a week meant completing take-home assignments: a stack of math sheets, a book report on Sacagawea, and a detailed journal describing her trip. With a sigh, she grabbed the journal like a lifeline, along with the new box of colored pencils she'd gotten for her art class. They'd just begun analyzing the works of the Mexican artist Frida Kahlo when she'd left for Pakistan. Frida's paintings were instantly recognizable by their bold, earthy colors—rainforest yellows, blood reds, vibrant blues, and neon pinks.

She flipped open the history book and froze. On the first page was a date, along with a signature: *Malik Humayun Ahmed*. Her grandfather. She stared at the blue ink, thinking back to a summer day, five years ago, when she'd gotten into a particularly nasty fight with Zara—over what, she couldn't remember. But it had ended how their fights usually did, with her sister throwing verbal daggers at her while she stood there mute, unable to formulate a good jab in response.

Later, it was *Nanabba* who'd coaxed Maya out of a tree and set up an easel for her in his office. Painting, for him, he'd explained, was like meditation. He'd shown her how to use a brush, demonstrating how the strokes could disentangle her thoughts. Each color, he told her, meant something different as it formed an image on the canvas. Red was danger, pink meant love, yellow hinted at cowardice, blue resonated calmness, green was renewal, and brown symbolized the earth. Maya fell in love with the process and later found that writing served the same purpose.

"And he was right." Maya sighed, writing a title on the front of her journal: "My Journey to Pakistan." On the next page she sketched a rectangular stretch of land, bordered by Afghanistan, India, China, and the Arabian Sea along the bottom. Then she began to write, soothed by the rush of words spreading across the page.

Thursday, September 15
Karachi, Pakistan

Here are some facts about Pakistan:
1. The name Pakistan—pak ("pure") and stan ("land") means "land of the pure" in the Persian and Urdu languages.
2. Islamabad is the capital, though Karachi is the biggest city.
3. The population is 193 million people, making

Pakistan the sixth most populous country in the world.

4. The national language is Urdu, the official language is English, and Saraiki, Punjabi, Pashto, Sindhi, and Baluchi are also spoken.

5. The official currency is the Pakistani rupee.

6. Cricket is the most popular sport.

My mom's family is from Karachi, Pakistan, but my dad was born in Chicago. His parents came to the United States from Pakistan in the 1970s so his father could get a PhD in engineering. As soon as he graduated, they moved to the West Coast and settled in Berkeley, California. My parents met when my dad went to Karachi to visit his grandparents. They liked each other instantly and decided to get married.

Maya paused. There was no avoiding it, she realized. Her grandfather was the reason they were here, and she had to say something about him.

The day before yesterday, my grandfather went to weed his garden in the cool part of the afternoon, as he usually did. A few hours later, that's where they found him, lying peacefully in a patch of tulips. He'd had a heart attack.

He was the eldest of three boys, and his greatest wish growing up was to fly. And so, even though his dad was totally against it, he became an air force pilot for the Pakistani military. But he didn't stay in the sky long. He came tumbling down to earth when he crashed during a training drill, and broke his back. His flying career over, he joined his father's accounting firm. When my grandfather told me this story, he wasn't sad. He just accepted what had happened as the will of God. He told me that as he buried his dream of flying, he uncovered something else—the joy of gardening.

My last memory is of him sitting on the porch, holding his pipe. I can still smell the smoke rising in the warm night air, mixed with the scent of musk and cedar wood—his Old Spice cologne. He'd been telling me one of my favorite stories about his childhood—about the time he and his best friend climbed up a mango tree and hung their schoolmaster's bicycle from its branches.

. . .

Maya exhaled a pent-up breath, the air rushing out of her lungs as her eyes filled with tears. She had been his favorite, she knew. He had never said it, but in his quiet, gentle way, he'd hinted at it as they both worked together on some shared interest or another— painting, gardening, collecting old coins, eating unripe mangoes sprinkled with chili pepper and salt. She clutched the journal to her chest and leaned back against the sofa, comforted by the words that were bringing her grandfather back to life, even if just for a moment.

Hot. It's really hot. Eyes flickering open, Maya found herself in a large four-poster bed with her sister sprawled beside her, a rumbling snore whistling through her nose. The window stood like a velvety black square, facing the garden. Jet-lagged, she must have conked out on the sofa and been moved here. She kicked off the too-warm blanket and sat up. *I should record her,* Maya thought gleefully, momentarily forgetting where she was. Her sister would have a conniption if she heard herself snoring. Maya sighed, staring at Zara's tranquil, pretty features, usually ani-mated and full of life. But the momentary thought of embarrassing her popular, perfect sister filled her with quiet satisfaction—it hadn't been easy growing up as her younger sibling.

A junior at Berkeley High, Zara came home with straight As and had just been elected captain of the debate team. At Sunday school at the local mosque, the teachers were always perplexed that Maya was Zara's younger sister, since she couldn't memorize the passages from the Quran as fast as her older sister could. She'd wanted to reply that she took her time to analyze what she was memorizing to understand it better, but as usual, she couldn't muster the courage to do so. Maya's hands twisted the blanket. It wasn't as if Zara went out of her way to be mean to her—it was just so hard growing up in her shadow. Maya felt like she was forever trying to reach her, figuratively and literally, since Zara also towered a good foot above her.

Maya glanced at the clock on the side table, which glowed 5:23. A grumble below her belly button reminded her that she hadn't eaten any dinner. A particular eater—or "picky," as her sister would describe her—she stuck to the few things she liked. Right now, toast with jam sounded perfect. *It's nearly noon back home,* she thought. If only none of this had happened and she could be in school with her friends, huddled over a lunch of her usual cheddar and tomato sandwich. Slipping from bed, she headed downstairs, through the dark hall leading to the kitchen. She felt for the door, twisted the knob, and stepped inside— and was enveloped in a rush of icy air redolent with the scent of roses . . . *definitely not the kitchen.*

Illuminated by the small coffee table lamp lay *Nanabba*, wrapped in crisp white sheets, covered by garlands of his favorite flower, *Rosa bourboniana.* They'd been cut from his garden, where they were in full bloom, after a good soaking from the monsoon rains. The glorious pink roses filled every nook and cranny of the small sitting room. In the morning he'd be taken to the morgue, then fly back with them to San Francisco to be buried. Her gaze fixed on the body, she crossed the threshold, pulling the door closed behind her.

As she listened to the hum of the air conditioner, cranked open on full blast to keep her grandfather's body cold, Maya stood in the shadow of a bookshelf, staring at the long, ghostly shape. Her toes curled against the marble floor. She just couldn't walk over to look at her *nanabba*'s face, which had been left exposed.

She turned her gaze toward the shelf, laden with pictures: a shot of her first birthday party, her face covered with cake; Zara's *Ameen* celebration when she'd finished reading the Quran in Arabic; her twin cousins after they were born; her aunt's graduation from Boston University; and a family picnic at the beach a few winters ago. Nestled in the center sat a small, faded color photo set in a silver frame. A giddy young couple stood in their wedding finery, eyes glowing. Instead of a traditional blood-red bridal dress, *Naniamma* had chosen a turquoise gown, setting tongues wagging and adding fuel to the gossip. *Nanabba* loved talking about the tumultuous events that had led up to the happy occasion; the story of their relationship had caused quite a scandal in the old days, as was usually the case when a young man from a wealthy family married a penniless orphan.

As Maya stared at the picture, taken nearly half a century before, she heard the door swing open. She shrank into the shadows, spotting a tiny shape float inside the room. It was *Naniamma*. At first, her grandmother paused; then she hurried over to her husband. Head bowed, she collapsed beside his body and clutched the corner of a sheet. As she cried, Maya averted her gaze, embarrassed to be spying. Although Maya and her grandmother were carbon copies of each other on the outside, sharing the same small frame, thick, wavy hair, and large gray-brown eyes, on the inside it was *Naniamma* and Zara who were two peas in a pod: outgoing, opinionated, and extremely stubborn when backed into a corner. As Maya huddled beside the bookshelf, she was torn by indecision; should she rush over and hug her or just give her some privacy? Zara would have rushed over. . . .

It was the clang at the front gate that made the decision for her. Not wanting to bother her grandmother, she slipped out the door and ran upstairs. The *chowkidar*, or guard, was letting in her aunt, Syeda *Khala*, who'd arrived from Chicago.

"Hey, Maya!" chorused the twins, Zaki and Ali, as they barreled through the dining room later.

"Hey," said Maya, putting down the butter knife to receive their exuberant hugs.

The boys had turned four a week before and were full of energy, since they'd slept most of the journey from Chicago.

Syeda *Khala*, on the other hand, looked like she hadn't slept in days. "Maya *jaan*," she said, giving her a kiss on her head. "How are you?"

"I'm fine," said Maya, watching her pour a cup of steaming tea.

"Where's Zara?" asked her aunt.

"Sleeping," replied Maya. "She always has a hard

time with the jet lag. It takes her a day to adjust."

"Syeda!" cried Maya's mother, entering the dining room.

"Oh, Dalia," wept Syeda *Khala*, her eyes spilling over with tears as she clutched her older sister. "I still can't believe *Abbu* is really *gone*."

"I know," said Dalia. "It was so unexpected—he was in such good health. It was *Ammi* I was more worried about, with her high blood pressure."

Realizing that her mother and aunt needed some privacy, Maya grabbed a stack of toast along with a jar of jam. "C'mon, guys," she said to her cousins. "We'll have a picnic and watch cartoons."

After breakfast, as mourners paraded through the house, Maya's youngest aunt, Sofia *Khala*, finally arrived from Little Rock, Arkansas, with her husband, Uncle Jad. Zara and Maya were tasked with keeping the boys busy upstairs in the television lounge while the adults huddled over stacks of papers and made phone calls. Zara had finally stumbled downstairs at noon and now sat nursing a cup of milky tea, laboriously taking notes from a thick biology book to keep up with classwork.

"I'm hungry," complained Ali, looking up from his coloring book.

"Me too," Zaki chimed in.

"Can you get them something?" mumbled Zara, waving her pen in Maya's direction.

Maya's nose flared at her sister's bossiness, but she held her tongue. She was kind of thirsty herself. Shutting her journal with a snap, she rose.

"Oh, I'll come down too," said Zara, taking her cup. "I need more sugar in my tea."

As they approached the kitchen door, the echo of strained voices floated toward them. Zara slowed, grabbing Maya's arm.

"What?" grumbled Maya in irritation, as her sister put her finger to her lips.

Zara stepped into the kitchen and pulled Maya into a hiding spot beside the bulky refrigerator.

"Alia *Bhabi*," said Great-Uncle Ahmed to *Naniamma*, his voice gravelly, "I know it's hard, but you must sell the house and take care of financial matters before your daughters leave."

"But this is all too soon," said *Naniamma*. "There is so much to do. . . ."

"*Ammi*," said Maya's mom soothingly, "we'll help you sort everything out. If things are left, Uncle Ahmed will take care of it."

"It's overwhelming for all of us," whispered

Sofia *Khala*, "but you and *Abbu* had already started planning your move to the United States to retire. Unfortunately, we just have to speed things up."

Maya crouched down to peer around the metal edge of the fridge and saw Uncle Jad gently patting his mother-in-law on the back.

"There was a fair offer on the villa from one of the neighbors," said Great-Uncle Ahmed, running a weary hand over his balding head. "Alia *Bhabi*, you should take it."

"He's right," said Sofia *Khala*. "Once news is out that *Abbu* is gone, crooks are going to come out of the woodwork to try and swindle you out of your home and possessions. The lawlessness in Karachi is increasing day by day and the political situation is very unstable, especially with elections around the corner."

"Yes," echoed Syeda *Khala*. "The cars will be easily sold, and we'll all help you get packed up."

"But what about our trip to India?" said *Naniamma*, out of the blue. "We were all going together in December, in less than three months."

A hush fell over the kitchen table. "*Ammi*, I don't think we can go," said Dalia.

"But you don't understand," said *Naniamma*, her voice strained. "I *must* go to India."

Maya stared at her grandmother, surprised that she still wanted to go to India, so soon after her grandfather's death.

"We've been trying to go to India for over forty years but the Indian government wouldn't give us visas!" cried *Naniamma*. "You know how difficult they make things for Pakistanis, especially those who've served in the military, like your father. We had to file special papers to get the right approvals and clearances. Finally we got our visas, and only after that could we purchase our tickets."

"Yes, *Ammi,* we know all the trouble he went through," said Sofia *Khala*, her voice breaking. "And we know what the trip means to you, but this is not a time to go looking for—"

"*Ammi*, they're right," interrupted Dalia. "We all got our passports stamped with Indian visas and bought our tickets too, but it's just not possible to go now. We have to leave for San Francisco in a week—*Abbu* needs to be buried. Already we are breaking tradition by not burying him within twenty-four hours of his death."

What does Naniamma want to look for in India? Maya wondered as her grandmother continued.

"Your father promised me. . . . It's been my dream

since I was a little girl," insisted *Naniamma*, sadness settling over her fine features as Syeda *Khala* tried to dab her tearstained cheeks with a crumpled tissue. "Once my visa expires, you know it will be impossible to get another one."

Hearing the desperation in her grandmother's voice, Maya felt her heart grow heavy. *This trip is really, really important to her.*

"I know, *Ammi*," said Dalia. "We were all looking forward to going, but we'll find another way to go, I promise."

At that moment, the cook came in from the market through the side door where the grown-ups sat, carrying a plastic bag from the butcher. With so many people in the house, he had been cooking nonstop. As he crossed the room, a line of blood trickled down along the tiled floor. Glimpsing the crimson puddle, *Naniamma* paled. She rose abruptly and turned to leave.

"Ammi," called out Sofia *Khala*, about to go after her, but Maya's mom grabbed her arm.

"This has all been a lot for her. Let her be."

Zara emerged from the hiding spot beside the fridge, about to say something, but their grandmother hurried past. Shoulders slumped, Zara joined the adults, but Maya inched toward the kitchen door, watching *Naniamma* grab her purse and head toward the garden. Gray clouds were building in the distance, a signal of an approaching monsoon shower.

Where is she going? Maya wondered. She followed, pausing at the door and watching as *Naniamma* rounded the fountain and hurried deeper into the garden, which was a riot of colorful blooms. *All shades of the rainbow except for red,* Maya thought. Once she'd disappeared behind the jasmine bushes, Maya slipped out the door and traced her footsteps, pausing on the opposite side of the foliage, breathing in the heady scent of the small white flowers. Through the foliage, she heard her grandmother unzip her purse and rummage inside. Maya's toes sank into the warm, moist soil as she leaned forward, catching a glimpse of silver—a cell phone.

"Muhi, it's me, Alia Auntie," said *Naniamma,* her voice tight with urgency. "I need you to do something for me . . . but please keep it *strictly* between us. . . ."

2

Secrets and Lies

As THE FAMILY GATHERED around the table for lunch, Maya sat between the twins, watching her grandmother remove a white pill from one of her medicine bottles and swallow it with a sip of water. Their grandmother's health had been deteriorating these past few years—that was one of the reasons she and *Nanabba* had decided to leave Karachi. Instead of reaching for the rice, chicken stew, or her favorite, sweet and sour potatoes, *Naniamma* plucked a guava from the fruit bowl. As she sliced through its green skin, revealing pink flesh studded with tiny seeds, she kept glancing at the clock on the wall.

At the other end of the table, Maya's mother and aunts huddled over a long list of things that needed to be done. Maya glanced from them to Zara, who gave her a knowing look. Maya ducked her head, staring at the untouched mound of rice on her plate. She didn't like eating chicken with bones in it, much to her mother's dismay. But she couldn't help it. Bones gave her the creeps.

The moment she'd overheard *Naniamma*'s secret, she'd realized she couldn't keep the knowledge to herself. With great reluctance she'd sought out her sister, who was slouching in the television lounge reviewing biology notes.

"Zara," said Maya, her voice barely audible.

"Uh-huh?" responded Zara, not bothering to look up.

"I need to talk to you. I think it's important. . . . It's about *Naniamma*," whispered Maya.

"What about her?" asked Zara, looking up, eyebrow raised.

"Well . . . ," said Maya, looking behind her to make sure no one was there. "I followed her into the garden after she left the kitchen. She got on the phone and spoke to someone named Muhi. She asked him to come over—with a ticket to India."

Understanding dawned on Zara's features. "She's sneaking off!"

Maya nodded. "It's been her dream to go, ever since she was a little girl."

"She was born there," said Zara with a knowing look.

"Really?" asked Maya, surprised. "I didn't know that. How did she end up here in Pakistan?"

"I don't really know *all* the details," said Zara, frowning. "I heard Mom and Syeda *Khala* talking about it once, and when I asked them, they never quite answered my question. Anyway, all I know is that she came to Pakistan and ended up in an orphanage. One of the teachers there noticed how smart she was and helped get her a scholarship to attend college. She was a senior, studying math, when *Nanabba* met her."

"Yeah, I know that part of the story," said Maya. "He saw her having an argument with the peanut vendor, who had tried to cheat her."

"Yeah," Zara said with a sad smile. "That's when he decided that this was the girl he was going to marry."

"He's the one who promised to take her to India," whispered Maya. "And now he's gone."

"We have to stop her," said Zara, sitting up. "People

do all sorts of crazy things when they're grieving."

"Should we tell Mom?" asked Maya.

"No, no." Zara shook her head with authority. "Mom has enough to worry about."

So now here they were, at the lunch table. Zara glanced up at the clock. Unusually quiet, she picked up her plate and snuck away to the kitchen. This was the signal. Maya stood, legs quivering. She slipped into the kitchen and spotted her sister standing impatiently at the back door.

"Move it, slowpoke," whispered Zara, pushing open the screen door.

"Coming," responded Maya. She wondered if what they were doing was the right thing. But Zara would go with or without her, and this was *her* secret and she had to see it through.

Zara exited the kitchen, nearly colliding with the planters filled with fresh herbs that sat outside the door. She sprinted across the driveway, Maya at her heels. They stopped beside the garage that loomed across from the front gate, and ducked between two parked cars. Five minutes later, *Naniamma* exited the main house and strode purposefully to the gate. Maya and Zara saw her hand the *chowkidar* a hundred rupees and heard her murmur something about picking up groceries at the corner store. He set off on his errand, and a few moments later, a portly figure sputtered up on a sky-blue Vespa.

"*Salaam Alaikum*, Alia Auntie," wheezed the young man, patting down his goatee, eyes sorrowful.

"*Walaikum Salaam*, Muhi," said *Naniamma*, glancing nervously over her shoulder. The girls crouched lower behind *Nanabba*'s old jeep.

"We heard about Malik *Sahib*," said Muhi. "My mother sends her condolences and promises to come by soon."

"Thank you, Muhi. It will be good to see her," said *Naniamma*, eyes darting down the road. "Do you have it?"

"Yes," he said, pulling out an envelope from his leather satchel. "But are you *sure* you want to do this?"

Maya and Zara shared anxious looks.

"Young man," said *Naniamma* in her stern school-teacher voice, "I will be fine."

"But, Alia Auntie," said Muhi, wringing his hands. "It's not safe. . . . Things have been tense between India and Pakistan since the bombings in Mumbai last year."

"But relations have improved," replied *Naniamma*.

"Our president was just in India, business between the countries has picked up, tourists are visiting, and India is even hosting a cricket match for the Pakistani national team—there's one taking place in a few days in Agra."

"True . . . ," muttered Muhi, "but it's still dangerous for a woman traveling alone."

"For heaven's sake," said *Naniamma*, exasperated. "I'm not naive."

Muhi's cheeks reddened. "It's my duty to tell you the dangers, Alia Auntie. My mother will never forgive me if something terrible happens to you."

Maya's heart raced as she absorbed the travel agent's words. She hadn't known there was so much animosity between the two countries.

"I've made up my mind, Muhi," said *Naniamma*, her voice unwavering. "My husband promised me we would go—he planned it for years. And now, well . . . I *must* go."

"We have to stop her," whispered Maya, tugging on her sister's arm. "Say *something*. . . . Make her stop!"

"But this trip really does mean a lot to her." Zara's face revealed conflicting emotions.

Maya's stomach sank as she saw a familiar look settle over her sister's face. Their father called it Zara's bullheaded-rhino look—the one she got whenever she had an idea from which she wouldn't budge.

"But she can't go alone . . . ," added Zara, shifting from one foot to another.

Before Maya could even think to stop her, Zara had jumped up from behind the jeep. *"Naniamma!"* she cried.

Muhi and her grandmother froze, but only for an instant. "Zara," scolded her grandmother. "What are you doing out here?"

"Naniamma, I'm sorry, I—I shouldn't have been snooping," stammered Zara. "But I couldn't help it. . . . I know what you're going to do."

"Jaan," said *Naniamma,* clearing her throat. "I don't know what you heard, but I think you are confused. . . ."

"No," said Zara. "You're going to India."

Maya huddled beside the jeep, surprised by her sister's brazenness. That was not the way you spoke to your elders.

"Go back to the house and forget what you heard," ordered their grandmother. "This is not something you need to involve yourself with."

Maya took in her grandmother's drooping shoulders and exhausted, red-rimmed eyes. *She just can't go on such a difficult trip by herself,* she thought.

"I have a better idea," said Zara. "How about I come with you?"

Maya stared openmouthed in shock. *Go with her?* They were supposed to stop her from going at all.

Muhi looked from Zara to *Naniamma* as if watching a tennis match.

Naniamma blinked, then said firmly, "Absolutely not."

"I won't be in the way, I promise," pleaded Zara.

Naniamma blinked again, as if considering the idea. "No, you cannot come with me, child."

Zara played her trump card. "If you don't let me go, I'm going to tell my mother what you're doing."

Naniamma went white, her lips compressed.

Slowly, legs shaking, Maya rose from her hiding spot, furious that her sister was getting her way again—and using *her* secret to get her way. Surprising even herself, she shouted, "If you're going, I'm going too!"

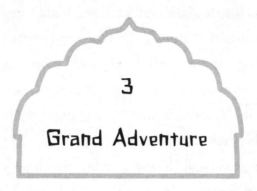

3

Grand Adventure

"We're going to miss our flight," muttered *Naniamma*, glancing over at the clock, glowing 4:46 in the early morning darkness. They'd been just about to sneak out when Syeda *Khala* had stumbled out of her room and wandered downstairs.

"Ow," muttered Maya, elbowing Zara, who had stepped on Maya's foot to peek around the door into the hallway.

After what seemed like an hour, Syeda *Khala* came back upstairs with a glass of water and disappeared into her room.

"Go *quietly*," instructed *Naniamma*, gingerly creeping down the stairs.

On the bottom step, Zara tripped. She would have tumbled into a glass cabinet if she hadn't grabbed on to the banister. "Sorry," she muttered, earning a disapproving glance from *Naniamma,* who had paused to prop up a note on the hall table. Without mincing words, she'd written that they'd gone to India and would be back in a few days.

Maya glanced at the crisp white envelope and shivered. Guilt settled over her like a heavy blanket as she followed Zara onto the front porch. The house was going to erupt in chaos the moment the letter was opened. Shrugging off the feeling of unease, she gulped in the cool night air and tiptoed across the driveway. Gently unlocking the squeaky metal gate, *Naniamma* ushered them onto the street of the affluent suburb where she lived. Maya scanned the street, holding her breath, expecting someone to come barging out after them, but the pale house stood silent, windows dark and shuttered.

Kalam, *Naniamma*'s loyal, burly driver of more than two decades, stood waiting. *Naniamma* had instructed him to park the small Suzuki down the street from the house the day before. The trio hurried toward it, the neighboring villas hunched over them, wrapped within concrete cocoons, slumbering against the inky sky. Other than a three-wheeled rickshaw sputtering past, there was no one else on the road. Maya had never seen Karachi so eerily quiet, but she knew that within an hour, the morning rush would pick up, and *Naniamma* wanted to be at the airport well before their eight a.m. flight.

"Kalam, we must hurry," said her grandmother, glancing at her watch for the hundredth time.

The driver stacked their luggage in the trunk while Maya slid into the backseat, escaping the early morning chill. Zara slid in next, followed by *Naniamma*, her small hands gripping her purse, a frown creasing her forehead. Maya's cheeks warmed as she recalled what had happened barely thirteen hours before: Zara's threats to reveal *Naniamma*'s plan . . . Maya insisting that she go to India too. Eventually, their grandmother's shoulders had slumped in defeat, and she'd asked Muhi to arrange for two additional airline tickets.

The rest of the day, Maya had flitted through the house, stomach in knots, secretly gathering things for their trip. *Naniamma* had told them to pack light: a change of clothes, sensible walking shoes, toiletries, and nothing else. Her tasks accomplished, Maya had sat in the corner of the living room, anxiously clutching her journal and the book on Pakistani history, watching her grandmother from the corner of her eye. *Naniamma* sat listening to her daughter's discussion with half an ear, then finally pleaded a headache and escaped to *Nanabba*'s office. To calm her anxiety, Maya flipped open her journal.

Friday, September 16
Karachi, Pakistan

My grandparents have always lived in Karachi, in a nice suburb called Clifton. Built along the Arabian Sea, Karachi is nicknamed the City of Lights because it never sleeps. It's home to twenty-three million people from different religious and ethnic backgrounds who came to find their fortune in Karachi's seaport and financial center.

My sister, who prides herself on knowing everything, and likes to rub it in when I don't, told me something that totally surprised me. I had thought that my grandmother, an orphan, was born in Karachi. But she wasn't. She was born in India. And her biggest wish in the world has always been to go back to visit. She and my grandfather had been trying to go for years, but I guess it's really hard for someone who served in the Pakistani military to get a visa.

Maya's hand shook as she wrote the last sentence. She stopped. Her heart wasn't in it. She wished she could write what was really on her mind. But that was impossible. She couldn't admit that she and Zara had pretty much blackmailed their grandmother into taking them to India with her. But now it was done, and they'd promised to help her. There was no backing out now.

Maya leaned against the car window, catching a last glimpse of the house as the engine hummed to life and they exited Clifton's Block 7. She glanced toward her grandmother, wanting to say *something* . . . to explain how sorry she was about how rude she and Zara had been yesterday. But once again, her tongue couldn't find the words. Too bad she couldn't just write her a note. She sighed, eyeing Zara, who usually had enough words for both of them. But Zara sat slumped in her seat, eyes closed. Frustrated, Maya turned to stare out the window, taking in the familiar sight of the suburbs where her grandparents lived. The multistoried Gulf Shopping Mall, where they often came to buy the latest fashion in *shalwar kameez*, passed by as they entered Saddar Town, one of the oldest parts of Karachi.

Their car jetted past a series of *jhuggis*, shantytowns, haphazardly constructed of scavenged wood, tin, and plastic sheeting. Many *jhuggis* dotted the city; they were where the majority of the city's poor lived, illegally squatting in empty lots.

Kalam maneuvered past a sad-eyed donkey pulling a cart laden with melons, toward a roundabout, a circular intersection around which traffic flowed. As the car went around the concrete curve, Maya saw tiny sets of feet protruding from beneath flattened cardboard boxes. Her heart clenched. They were street children, huddling together for warmth and protection on the concrete island. They would be up at dawn, she knew, working along the dangerous road, selling trinkets or cleaning windows for a few rupees. Whenever Maya went shopping in the bazaars, her mother tightly gripped her hand, fearful she'd get lost, or worse. It was not uncommon for children to be kidnapped and used by gangs to steal or beg on the streets; the newspapers often reported on children being maimed, their arms and legs mutilated and cut off so that they would get more money, out of pity.

The sleeping children disappeared in the side-view mirror as a set of stone towers stood ahead, rising from the Holy Trinity Church. Kalam turned left onto Elphinstone Street, its colors coming to life in the early morning light. As Maya eyed the shops, filled with rich tapestries and heavy carpets tucked into ornate Gothic buildings from the mid-nineteenth century, she thought how the colors of the city never failed to amaze her. The pinks were more pink, the yellows and oranges electrifying, blues bright, and greens eye-catching.

"After your grandfather left the air force, he worked in that office," said *Naniamma* absentmindedly, staring at a limestone building with stately arches, nestled between the English Boot House and a restaurant that was a family favorite, Bundoo Khan's Kabob House.

Maya and Zara shared an anxious glance as their grandmother continued, lost in old memories. "I'd visit him after I finished teaching at Mama Parsi School, and we'd get kebabs for dinner."

"I love Bundoo Khan's kebabs too," said Zara, then

pressed her lips together as if remembering it probably wasn't a good idea to speak.

Maya exhaled a pent-up sigh, silently agreeing with her sister, since kebabs were on her approved-foods list. But she was just relieved that *Naniamma* was speaking to them at all. *Maybe her anger is fading,* she thought hopefully.

As if beginning to forgive them, just a little, *Naniamma* gave them a tired smile. "Over sixty years ago, Bundoo arrived from India and started his business as a simple street stall, selling kebabs and his marvelous, flaky *paratha* bread. Now they have restaurants all over—even in Dubai, London, and Chicago."

Kalam merged onto Jinnah Terminal Road. "Looks like a precaution for the upcoming elections," he said, slowing at a roadblock manned by gun-toting guards, who waved them through.

Naniamma harrumphed with irritation. "Some elections. Corrupt, money-grubbing politicians fighting for power, not paying a hoot to the needs of the people."

"Yes, *Baji*," agreed Kalam, pulling up alongside the sprawling airport. "Things have only gotten worse over the years, especially now that religious extremists like the Taliban are causing chaos with shootings and bombings."

"Well, you keep safe while I'm away," said *Naniamma*, opening the car door. "When my daughters learn that I'm gone, they will question you. Let them know that you only did as I asked, and that you will pick me up in four days when I return."

Maya glanced anxiously down at her watch; her mother was going to be up soon, and Maya could just imagine the ruckus when she found the letter. *No turning back now. . . .* Kalam placed their luggage on a cart and a porter guided them into Jinnah airport.

"You're cutting it close," said the mustached clerk, quickly scanning their passports for visas and processing their luggage. "You must hurry; your flight will be boarding soon," he said, handing them their boarding passes as they hurried toward the security gates.

They were about to pass through, when their grandmother froze. A bronze plaque stood facing them, engraved with a familiar aquiline profile of a man wearing a trademark Karakul hat, and a simple inscription: *Mohammed Ali Jinnah, Founder of Pakistan, December 25, 1876–September 11, 1948.*

Naniamma stared wide-eyed at the portrait, pity and sorrow lining her face.

"What's wrong?" Zara asked softly.

As if she hadn't heard her, *Naniamma* rushed on through security.

With their grandmother between them, Maya fiddled with her seat belt while Zara folded her lanky frame into the aisle seat. The pilot's voice crackled above them, requesting that they fasten their seat belts. With surprising efficiency, the plane sped up the runway and, with a burst of power, took off. Eyes squeezed shut, *Naniamma* leaned back in her seat, gripping the armrests.

The sisters stared at each other, neither quite believing that they were going to India. Maya frowned, and then glanced pointedly at their grandmother, silently urging Zara to say something, anything, to make up for their awful behavior the day before.

Zara gave a helpless shrug.

Say something! mouthed Maya.

"Naniamma," Zara finally began, her usually booming voice subdued. "I'm really, really sorry I was so disrespectful yesterday . . . that we forced you to bring us to India."

Naniamma's eyelids flickered open as Maya nodded vigorously in agreement.

Her grandmother slowly looked from one sister to the other as her lips revealed a hint of a smile. "I accept your apology," *Naniamma* said, then paused. "Though I'm still questioning my judgment for letting you come."

Maya ducked her head, embarrassed.

"Your mother is going to be furious. Can you imagine how she'll react when she sees that letter?"

For once, Zara sat tongue-tied, looking for the right thing to say. Before she could come up with anything, her grandmother hid her face with her hands, shoulders shaking.

"Naniamma," whispered Maya, reaching over to hug her. "It's not your fault."

But instead of tears, there came a peal of muffled laughter. Surprised, Maya sat back.

"It seems that we are three peas in a pod, you two and me," said *Naniamma*, revealing a shameful grin. "Stubborn as goats!"

Relieved, the sisters giggled, feeling the tension ease. Elation flooded through Maya. For once she felt as if she was one of them—brave, adventurous, and officially one of the peas!

Zara took *Naniamma*'s hand. "I've been dying to ask. . . . Why is this trip so important to you?" Maya leaned in to hear the answer to the question that had been gnawing at her as well, while her sister added, "We know that you came to Pakistan when you were a little girl and ended up in an orphanage. What happened to your family?"

All traces of laughter evaporated as *Naniamma* looked from one granddaughter to the other, brown-gray eyes clouded with uncertainty.

"Are you okay?" asked Maya. "Should I get you some water?"

Her grandmother sighed. "No, no," she said, clasping each girl's hand in her own. "Now that both of you are my partners in this adventure, I think I need to tell you the entire story. From the beginning."

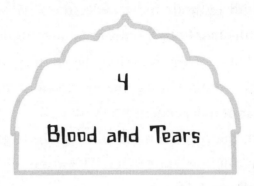

4

Blood and Tears

NANIAMMA'S EYES TOOK ON a faraway look, as if she were watching an old movie whir to life in the back of her mind. "My father was a well-respected doctor in a township called Aminpur, in India," she began. "Our family had lived there for generations."

Maya's eyes widened. She had never heard about *Naniamma*'s father.

"It was 1947—I was seven and World War II had ended a few years before. The entire world was changing, and in the midst of the upheaval, India was also in turmoil. For nearly three hundred years it had been a colony of the British, the jewel in their vast empire."

"Oh, like America's thirteen British colonies," said Maya, without even realizing it.

"Yes, something like that," said *Naniamma*. "But the British came to India under the guise of doing trade as the East India Company. Slowly, using private armies, they took power over the country. In retaliation, Indians rose up in mutiny all over India in the 1857 war of independence."

"Well, the American colonists rebelled against the English king too," said Zara. "They dumped British tea into Boston Harbor and George Washington led the Revolutionary War to gain independence from King George."

"Sadly, the Indian rebellion was not so successful," said *Naniamma*. "The British deposed the great Mughal emperor and took over most of the country. Over the next hundred years, Indians protested, marched, and fought for independence. I'm sure you've heard of Mahatma Gandhi. He used nonviolent means to fight the British—there were many brave men and women like him."

Maya listened with rapt attention. No one had ever told her any of this. "Did they fight a revolutionary war like the Americans?"

"In the end, there was no war," said *Naniamma*,

her lips compressed for a moment. "The British were broke after World War Two, so they pretty much gave up and fled the country . . . but not before forcing the people to make a life-changing decision."

"What kind of decision?" asked Zara.

"You have to understand a bit of history," said *Naniamma* with a deep sigh. "For thousands of years, India was the most ethnically, culturally, and religiously diverse country in the world. When Mark Twain visited in 1895, he said that 'in religion, India is the only millionaire.'"

"He wrote *Huckleberry Finn*," said Zara in surprise. "We read it in English class."

"When the British arrived, they used a practice called 'divide and conquer,'" said *Naniamma*. "They categorized Indians by religion—Hindu, Muslim, Sikh, Jew, Christian, Buddhist, and Zoroastrian—sowing disputes among them to keep them apart."

"Wow," muttered Zara.

"Even though the various communities had differences before the British arrived, they had lived mostly in harmony for centuries," explained *Naniamma*. "I remember when our Hindu or Sikh neighbors had a wedding, they would send over baskets of sweets. When my aunt got married, we sent snacks to Dr.

Tripathi, my father's Hindu colleague, whose daughter Reshma was my best friend in school."

The flight attendant came by with the drink trolley. *Naniamma* asked for tea, while the girls got orange juice. The flight attendant placed the cup in front of *Naniamma*, and they watched the steam rise from the swirling brown liquid.

"Even tea was introduced to us by the British," she said. "They stole the plant from China and grew it in India to break the Chinese monopoly."

"You love tea, *Naniamma*," said Maya, smiling.

"Well, it's one of the good things they did," she grumbled, adding milk and sugar to her cup. She paused a moment to look through her purse and frowned. "Looks like in my hurry I forgot my blood pressure medicine."

"Oh," said Zara. "Will you be okay?"

"I'm sure I can get some pills in Delhi. But my mind is wandering and I need to get back to the story. Where was I?"

"It was 1947," repeated Maya, "and the British decided to leave India."

"Yes," said *Naniamma*. "Up till then, the Indian leaders had let go of religious differences to fight their common enemy. But when they realized that the British were leaving, they began fighting among themselves, positioning themselves to take power. The Hindus, the majority of the population, clashed with Muslims, the largest minority."

Maya blinked in fascination. "So after three hundred years the British just got up and *left*?"

"Well," said *Naniamma*, "they'd planned a gradual transition paced over the course of a year, but the foolish governor of India, Lord Mountbatten, announced that they'd be gone in three months."

"Oh," said Maya. That seemed like an awfully short time to pack up and leave an entire country. She imagined the English packing up cardboard boxes filled with souvenirs and taking off.

"Anxiety and fear at the news spread through the streets of India," said *Naniamma*.

"Why weren't the people happy?" asked Maya.

"Don't be silly, Maya," said Zara with a sniff of superiority. "Can you imagine how scared the people were?"

"Yes, *jaan*," said *Naniamma*. "There was too much at stake for the Indian leaders to just be happy—they wanted power. Jinnah, the leader of the Muslim League, proposed a compromise on how the religious communities could coexist in a united India.

He wanted a weak central government so that the regions with religious minorities had more authority. But Nehru, the Hindu leader of the Congress Party, insisted on a strong central state."

"Mohammed Ali Jinnah?" said Maya, remembering the plaque at the airport.

"Yes," said *Naniamma*. "When Nehru rejected the compromise, Jinnah threatened to form a separate Muslim nation. He ordered a 'day of action' in Calcutta, but the peaceful march turned into a day of death; five thousand people were killed in clashes while British troops hid in their barracks. The violence quickly spread to the neighboring states of Bihar and Uttar Pradesh, but by this time none of the leaders, not even Gandhi who walked barefoot through the country, pleading for calm, could stop it. In the end, a British lawyer, Radcliffe, arrived with the task of carving up the country, and he did: the majority Muslim areas became Pakistan and the rest remained India."

"What?" gasped Maya. She'd heard grown-ups talking about India and Pakistan—the details were always fuzzy, and she hadn't paid much attention. "So Pakistan didn't exist before then?"

Zara rolled her eyes and sipped her juice.

"No," said *Naniamma*. "With the stroke of a pen, the Great Partition began and the country exploded in violence. Neighbors turned on one another, looting, burning, killing, and worse. . . . Families left villages they had lived in for generations and fled with barely the clothes on their backs. Muslim families, such as mine, had a critical decision to make."

Zara looked surprised.

"We had to decide whether to stay in India, as many Muslims did, or make the perilous journey to Pakistan, while Hindus and Sikhs traveled the opposite route, to India."

"And your family decided to leave?" asked Zara gently, taking their grandmother's hand.

"At first my father and his brothers couldn't agree what to do," said *Naniamma*, her eyes clouded with memories. "For days they debated, feeling as if they were being torn in two. In the end, our entire family decided we would go to Pakistan, and if things didn't work out, we would come back. So we packed up our family house in Aminpur, but my mother didn't want to take our valuables, in case we were robbed, so she hid them. Then my father, mother, three older sisters, and I got into our car and were driven by Dr. Tripathi to the train station. Once on the train, we squeezed into a compartment and barred the door." *Naniamma* stopped to take a sip of tea, while Maya shared an amazed look with her sister.

"We arrived in Delhi," continued *Naniamma*, "where my uncles and their families joined us. The train started moving again and things were fine until we arrived in the city of Amritsar, near the new Pakistan-India border. A group of men climbed aboard . . . and I don't remember anything after that."

"But you got to Pakistan," Maya burst out, unable to hold in her curiosity. "What happened to your parents, your sisters, aunts, uncles, and cousins?"

"When the train pulled into Lahore, no one disembarked," said *Naniamma*.

Maya gulped, the orange juice turning to acid in her stomach. She had to lean closer to her grandmother to hear her whispered words. "When the train conductor climbed on board, he found the aisles and compartments flowing with blood. Only three people on that train were alive, and one of them was me."

5

Delhi Landing

Saturday, September 17
Approaching Indian airspace

Here are some facts about India:

1. India is officially known as the Republic of India.

2. It has the second largest population in the world, with over 1.2 billion people.

3. Many different languages are spoken but the main ones are Hindi, Bengali, Telugu, Marathi, Tamil, and Urdu.

4. The capital is New Delhi, and the most populated city is Mumbai.

5. The official currency is the Indian rupee.

6. The most popular sport is cricket.

We will be landing in Delhi soon. The city is located where the Ganges and Indus Rivers meet. This area has been inhabited for a really, really long time—since the 3rd century BC. It's the spot where two families, the Kauravas and Pandavas, went to war. They're so famous that their story was written down as an epic Sanskrit poem, called the Mahabharata. Since then, Delhi has gone on to be the capital of many rulers, from the Muslim Mughals to the British.

Maya glanced up from her journal toward her grandmother and Zara, both asleep. *Naniamma*'s story had left them all teary eyed and exhausted. But Maya couldn't sleep. She turned back to the journal.

You might be wondering why we're on our way to Delhi. Well, it's been my grandmother's dream to go, and since we already had our *visas, we decided to come, just the three of us. My sister asked my grandmother why it was so important to go now, right after our grandfather's death. I'm glad she asked. I was too nervous. My grandmother's mother hid a chest at their old house. It contains her family's treasures! We're going on a treasure hunt! But what <u>Naniamma</u> really wants is a special ring to bury with <u>Nanabba</u>. I don't quite get what's so urgent about finding this ring, but <u>Naniamma</u> says it's important. She's so sad, it's probably wise not to question her too much.*

Maya reread what she'd written. It sounded pretty lame, she thought, but it was the best she could do, considering she couldn't fully grasp the truth. After learning so many family secrets, writing them down relieved the pressure in her head, so she continued.

I still can't get my head around the fact that my grandmother was one of millions of people who tried to cross the new border between

India and Pakistan. Her family were among the million who died.

But these people, who I never knew existed, were my family too. And they were Indian, so I guess that makes me a quarter Indian. I feel like I've discovered a part of myself that was hidden. Well, I can go home and tell Kavita, "Hey, I'm Indian too." Boy, will she be confused!

The FASTEN YOUR SEAT BELT signs flickered on, and the pilot cheerily announced that they were now over Delhi. Maya shut the journal as a thought struck her: *I'm part Indian, but before August 14, 1947, everyone was Indian.* Her nose pressed against the plane window, Maya gazed down at the sprawling city she had just been writing about, startled by its lush greenness. Wide swaths of parks and forests rubbed up against scabs of urban development stretching in all directions.

Maya followed her sister and grandmother from the plane, clutching her backpack, overwhelmed that she'd arrived in a country where they were foreign . . . *unwelcome.* At passport control, the official's bushy eyebrows scrunched together as he scrutinized *Naniamma*'s Pakistani passport. He glanced at her and her picture, but when he saw her place of birth—Aminpur, India— his brows relaxed.

"Ugh," grumbled Zara, fanning her face with a magazine as they stood at the edge of a huge crowd.

Maya frowned. The weather was exactly like Karachi's, hot and muggy. As her grandmother called out for a taxi through the clamor of voices, Maya looked around nervously, ears tuning into the conversations around them. Surprised, she realized that she could understand many of the words rushing past. Much of it was in accented English, a legacy left from colonial rule, she guessed. Some dialects were incomprehensible, but she deciphered much of the chatter, though some of the words sounded a bit different since the Hindi being spoken around her was a cousin of Urdu.

They clambered into an air-conditioned taxi and fell silent as they watched out the window. Maya saw three-wheel rickshaws, identical to the ones back in Karachi, and thought of Kavita, whose family was from Bangalore, India. They often spent the night at each other's house and never had she overheard anything bad about Pakistan from her or her parents. On the contrary, when they'd met in kindergarten they'd formed an instant bond, feeling like brown kindred spirits who shared a love of funny black-and-white movies and spicy fried *pakoras*, and a repulsion for wearing tight, sequined *shalwar kameez* outfits on special occasions. *India . . . Pakistan . . .* For them, they'd just been names of countries their parents came from, and that they sometimes visited over vacation, occasionally returning with stomach problems after eating something they weren't supposed to.

The impatient ringing of a cell phone broke through Maya's thoughts. It was coming from Zara's purse. Her sister pulled out her hot pink phone, a present for her fourteenth birthday. "It's probably Mom," she whispered, showing them the flashing number from *Naniamma*'s house in Karachi. "It looks like the SIM card I put in in Karachi for local calls works in India too. What do I do?"

"Pick it up, *jaan*," said *Naniamma* with a deep sigh. "There is no point in avoiding the inevitable."

Zara pushed the button to accept the call but was too late. It had rolled over into voice mail. "I'm sure she'll call again," she said, shoving it back in her purse. But not before the phone resonated with a deep buzz. The sisters shared an anxious glance. It was a text. From Mom.

Ignoring it, they went back to staring out the window.

The driver exited the airport and took the first right off the roundabout. "Where are you coming from?" he asked, glancing back at them via the rearview mirror, his eyes thickly lined with black kohl.

Naniamma was silent, then said quietly, "From Pakistan."

"Oh ho, Pakistan," said the driver warmly. "Welcome, welcome. Is this your first time?"

"No," said *Naniamma*. "I'm coming back after many years."

"Well, then, we have been having good weather," he said, exiting the airport. "Bit rainy, but good. The mangoes are delicious this season. . . ."

As he chatted on, Maya stared out the window, looking for something, anything, that proclaimed that they were now in a foreign land—*India*. But the reverse was true. A sense of familiarity settled over her as their taxi overtook a rickshaw, then sped past an elegant European sedan and a donkey cart. The faces that swam past her on the expressway ranged from pale cream to mahogany, and the people wearing familiar *shalwar kameezes* or jeans or suits could have easily been back in Karachi. The main difference was that the billboards and signs were in Hindi, its square script different from the flowing letters of Urdu.

They passed a series of large malls and multistory office buildings and stopped at a light. Beside them sat a husband and wife on a white Vespa, clutching three little kids. Maya grinned, thinking that India's seat belt laws must be as lenient as Pakistan's. As the taxi's meter whirred, counting the fare, the driver exited onto a wide, leafy boulevard. The driver pointed out a series of parks, mansions, and administrative offices that had been built to house and entertain the British during their reign.

As the driver slowed at an intersection, Zara pointed out the window. "Hey, isn't that Gandhi?"

Maya peered over her sister's shoulder, staring at the black sculpture of a familiar stooped figure in a loincloth, leading a group of people.

"It's the Dandi March," said *Naniamma*. "He led freedom fighters against oppressive salt taxes imposed by the British."

"Yes, madame," said the taxi driver, noticing their interest. "This sculpture was put in front of the President's House, which was formerly occupied by British officials."

"He fought against the British with such grace,"

sighed *Naniamma*, "but an assassin's bullet took his life soon after independence."

"Who killed him?" asked Zara, who'd pulled out her phone to take a picture.

"Nathuram Godse," said *Naniamma*.

The driver looked back with a nod. "Yes, madame knows," he added with a glower. "Nathuram was a member of a Hindu nationalist group, the RSS. He felt Gandhi betrayed them by giving the Muslims a separate country."

Maya stared at Gandhi's bespectacled, smiling face with a pang of sorrow as the taxi continued past the President's House, a columned mansion with sprawling gardens. Just down the road, past the Nehru Memorial Museum, rose their destination: the majestic pink sandstone Taj Palace Hotel. As Maya followed Zara from the taxi, she stumbled at the sight of a group of street children being shooed away by the hotel's efficient security guards. Before she could see where they'd gone, the doorman had whisked them inside. In another few minutes, their passports and reservation had been reviewed and they were being escorted to their room on the fifth floor.

• • •

An hour later, Maya sat eating toast and jam while her sister finished off the *akoori*, spicy scrambled eggs, at the small table overlooking the swimming pool from their room. She eyed the eggs, which she never ate. The texture was too weird—chewy and spongy at the same time. Their grandmother lifted her purse and gently removed a sheet of graph paper and smoothed it out on the table. Maya stared at the rows of bulleted points, diagrams, and tiny pictures drawn with a careful hand.

"What's that?" asked Zara, before Maya could open her mouth.

"This is my memory map," *Naniamma* said, her eyes beginning to glow with excitement.

"Memory map?" asked Maya, elbowing her sister in irritation.

"They are the things I remember from my life in India."

"What's it for?" asked Zara.

"I've created a map using my memories as markers, leading to the chest my mother hid before we fled."

"You remember where it is?" asked Maya, stomach aflutter.

"Of course," said *Naniamma*. "I helped her dig the hole under a guava tree in the back garden."

"I know you said you wanted to find the chest, but

why is it so important?" asked Zara, echoing Maya's thoughts.

Naniamma paused, her eyes still, staring off toward the rain-smeared window. "When I was growing up in the orphanage, the image of my parents became a blur in my mind," she whispered. "I've forgotten their faces . . . the shape of their noses, how they wore their hair."

Maya shivered. She couldn't imagine not knowing what her parents looked like or what it must have felt like to be alone in the world.

"My mother, according to family tradition, had four rings made, for each of her daughters. They were betrothal rings to be given to our husbands on our engagement day. But," she continued with a hollow chuckle, "I came to your *Nanabba* penniless, without family or possessions. So it became my life's obsession, if you will, to find the chest containing my family's treasures. No matter how long it took the Indian government to give us a visa, I was going to come so that I could put one of those rings on your grandfather's finger and show him where I came from and connect him to my family."

"But, *Naniamma*," said Zara in a whisper. "*Nanabba* can't wear a ring now, or see the photos."

With a glare, Maya elbowed her sister for her insensitivity. Realizing her mistake, Zara clapped her hand over her mouth. "I'm so sorry," she said. "I shouldn't have said that."

"Don't worry, *jaan*. I know he is gone." A determined glint had appeared in *Naniamma*'s eye. "But before he's laid to rest, I want him to have a ring on his finger, to keep always. Plus," explained their grandmother, "there are other links to our past in that old box—photographs, letters, jewelry, a Quran containing our family tree, and other heirlooms handed down for generations, worth far more than their monetary value. It's the only connection to my family that I have left—something I can bequeath to you so you know where our family comes from."

Excitement ran like quicksilver through Maya's veins. Maya knew that *Nanabba* would have wanted *Naniamma* to look for her family's lost treasures.

"We really are going on a treasure hunt," she breathed.

Naniamma laughed. "Yes, a treasure hunt of sorts. But first we're going back to where my journey to Pakistan began—to my uncle's house in Chandni Chowk, in the heart of Old Delhi," she said, pointing at the list. A series of streets crisscrossed the top left corner of the paper, drawn with a neat hand, each labeled with a remembered landmark. An X marked the spot beside a square labeled "Sunehri Masjid," or "golden mosque." Behind it stretched a squiggle of a lane labeled "Naughara Lane." "My uncle's neighbor was an old family friend, Mir Hayat. The keys and the deeds to our house were left with him for safe-keeping."

"You still know someone in Delhi?" asked Zara, amazed at the news.

"Well, he's probably passed on, but his family must still be there."

"How can you be sure?" asked Maya, before she could stop herself. She didn't want to dampen her grandmother's enthusiasm.

"Mir Hayat and his brothers swore on their great-grandfather's grave they would never leave Delhi," said *Naniamma*. "You see, they're descended from one of the oldest families in the city and have several bookbinding businesses in the bazaar. They wouldn't have left any of that for all the tea in China. So freshen up—there's no time to waste."

6

Down Memory Lane

THE TRIO STEPPED FROM the hotel onto a sidewalk cleansed and cooled by the monsoon showers. With springs in their steps, they strode down the sidewalk, looking for an open-air rickshaw, since *Naniamma* didn't want to be cooped up in a taxi. They paused at the corner to allow a group of smartly dressed families to stroll toward a small building nestled beside the hotel. Heads bowed, the group entered the turquoise structure, decorated with six pointed stars.

"'Judah Hyam Synagogue,'" read Zara, pausing at the sign.

"Jews arrived in India two thousand years ago,

after their temple in Jerusalem was destroyed," said *Naniamma*, admiring the building. "The king gave them a set of copper plates, granting them the right to live freely and build their places of worship."

Mark Twain sure wasn't kidding, thought Maya, giving the synagogue a last glance as they walked on. *India does seem to be the home to a million religions.*

Crowded in the backseat of a rickshaw, with Zara leaning precariously out over the edge to take pictures, they journeyed toward Connaught Place, a huge circle with roads spreading out like the spokes on a wheel. Maya had read up in the guidebook and found out that this part of Delhi, New Delhi, had been designed by the English architect Lutyens as the seat of British colonial government. They sputtered past a metro station, trendy boutiques, a McDonald's and Pizza Hut, cafés, and sleek office buildings marked with names of familiar companies. Soon the streets began to narrow and grow bumpier as they left New Delhi behind. As the rickshaw pulled up to a red light, Maya looked down and froze. They were surrounded by children in ragged clothes, some selling flowers and balloons, others with their hands out, begging. Maya remembered the kids sleeping on the roundabout in Karachi, and before she could take a few coins from her jean pocket, the rickshaw rattled on.

The children momentarily forgotten, Maya followed the line of her grandmother's intense stare, catching sight of a majestic dome looming up ahead.

"I so wanted to show your grandfather this . . . ," whispered *Naniamma*.

"What is it?" asked Zara, craning her neck.

"It's Jama Mosque, the largest mosque in India," said *Naniamma*, knuckles white as she gripped the edge of the seat. "My father took me and my sisters to see it one summer. . . . I remember counting the steps as we climbed to the north gate—three hundred eighty-nine. We were out of breath when we reached the top."

Maya imagined a man gently guiding a gaggle of giddy young girls up the steps. As the three sat in the rickshaw, lost in their own thoughts, the driver pulled aside at a towering three-story structure, stretching half a city block. The dull pink stone was set with semi-octagonal towers with lotus flowers carved into the horseshoe-shaped arch rising at its base.

"This is it, madame," said the driver. "Lahore Gate, like you asked."

Naniamma paid the driver and they stepped down

to face the imposing gateway. "This leads to Chandni Chowk, the city's busiest market," she said, eyes darting through the arched passageway. "From here we used to walk or take a bullock cart to Sunehri Masjid, the Golden Mosque. My uncle's house was behind it."

"Let's go," said Zara, brimming with confidence and optimism.

They passed through the gate and emerged into the bustling artery that led to the edge of Chandni Chowk. For a long moment they stood in the shadow of the gate, clutching one another's hands, their senses overpowered by the colorful sights and sounds. A medley of little shops stretched along the road, overflowing with kitchen supplies, stationery, linens, and cell phone accessories.

A traffic jam played out before them, a cacophony of horns, snarls of scooters, sputtering rickshaws, and sinewy men pulling carts laden with brass pots, electronic parts, and dry goods. Men and women wove between the vehicles, rushing to meetings; housewives carried baskets of vegetables; and street vendors and hawkers sold everything from phone cards to bags of neon-colored cotton candy. Maya inhaled a mixture of car exhaust and the scent of melons from a stall across the street and watched the chaos.

A tiny figure clad in a light blue sari, *Naniamma* stood wide-eyed and pale. "It's changed so much," she said, her voice a little uncertain. In her hand she clutched the sheet of graph paper—her memory map.

"Does anything look familiar?" asked Zara.

Before their grandmother could answer, a young man with a faint mustache stopped in front of them, carrying a tray of plastic combs. "Madame, you want?"

Naniamma shook her head and said emphatically, "No, thank you."

He shrugged and moved on. The vendor was replaced by another one, hawking potato chips. "Where you from?" he said. "You are not from here, no? Where? America? England?"

Naniamma grabbed the girls' hands and hurried across the street.

"How did he know?" Zara asked in surprise, echoing Maya's thoughts.

"They can tell from your clothes," she said distractedly. "They recognize they're foreign—your shoes, too."

Oh, wow, thought Maya, jumping back as a passing cart splashed dirty water in their direction.

"Now, stay close," warned their grandmother as she stopped beneath the awning of a spice shop. "Ignore anyone who tries to sell you something or tries to offer you help without you asking for it."

Maya nodded as their grandmother stared down at the memory map. "We go up this road until we come to a fountain," she said.

"What kind of fountain?" asked Zara.

"It's an old Victorian fountain," explained *Nania-mma*. "Made of carved marble."

"Like the ones people have in their garden?" asked Maya softly. "With flowing water?"

Naniamma paused, doubt flashing in her eyes. "Well, yes, kind of like that. It was just a small fountain. In a park."

"So we're looking for a park, too?" asked Zara.

"Yes, with benches and a stretch of grass. I remember having picnics there with my uncles and cousins."

Led by their grandmother, they plunged into a stream of bodies jostling up the street. They skirted a barber cutting his customer's hair on the sidewalk and took a left past a tree that Zara nearly ran into, since she was busy trying to take a picture of a cow sitting in the middle of the road blocking traffic.

"This was once the grandest bazaar in India," said *Naniamma*, eyeing the line of drooping shop fronts. "A pool sat at its center, reflecting the moon—that's what 'Chandni Chowk' means: 'moonlight square.'"

Squinting past the peeling paint, cracked wooden lattices, and broken balustrades, Maya tried to imagine what it must have looked like once. Her eyes widened as she caught hints of beauty: in the curve of wrought-iron balconies, intricately carved columns, and ornate cornices. She realized that this area must once have been quite posh—filled with ornamented palaces, elegant mosques, coffeehouses, and gardens. But now it had been swallowed up and run down. At the next intersection, *Naniamma* stood at the corner looking from her map up toward a small hotel across the street.

"It should be here," she muttered. She glanced at her memory map, looking confused.

Maya wondered uncomfortably how accurate *Naniamma*'s memory map was, plus how much had changed in the decades since her grandmother had been gone.

"Excuse me," said Zara, taking charge as she called out to a man exiting a television repair shop. "Can you tell us where the old Victorian fountain is?"

"It was torn down years ago, miss," said the man. "They built that hotel over it."

"Uh, thanks," said Zara. The man nodded and walked on.

"Oh, no," muttered Maya, a sinking feeling in her stomach. She looked at her grandmother, who was staring from the hotel down to her map, looking lost. *We need to help,* she thought. *We promised to find the chest for her, to get the ring for* Nanabba. Even Zara looked at a loss for words. Without thinking twice, Maya reached into her backpack and pulled out the guidebook. "*Naniamma,*" she said, "how about we try to match the landmarks in your memory map to a more current map of the area?"

Zara gave Maya a rare appreciative smile. "That's an *awesome* idea."

"Yes," said *Naniamma,* the lines around her mouth easing. "That would be very helpful, *jaan.*"

Zara reached for the guidebook, but Maya's finger tightened around its edges. "No," said Maya, surprising them both. "I'll navigate."

Zara paused, about to say something, but stopped. She stared at Maya, as if seeing her for the first time. "Okay, find Lahore Gate; that's where we came in."

Maya grabbed a colored pencil, forest green, symbolizing good luck, and flipped to a map of Old Delhi. The trio bent over the book, poring over the streets and alleys until Maya pointed out the gate's location and circled it.

"Where did you say your uncle's house was?" asked Zara.

"Behind Sunehri Masjid," replied her grandmother.

Maya examined the map key. "Sunehri Mosque is number seven on the map."

"There," Zara pointed out a second later. Maya circled it. "But the old Victorian fountain isn't on the map," Zara added with a frown.

"It's okay." Maya grinned with growing confidence. "We just need to find another landmark to orient ourselves. We can trace a route to the mosque from there."

"We'll need to backtrack a bit," said Zara, turning them around toward the gate.

"I remember this temple," said *Naniamma* excitedly, after they had walked a few blocks. She paused within a cloud of smoky-sweet incense wafting from the doorway of a Hindu temple.

Maya stared into the vast courtyard, where half a dozen statues stood, dressed in silks and draped with garlands of marigold and jasmine. A bright blue figure at the center caught her attention. "Which god is that?"

"Lord Rama," said *Naniamma*. "Beside him is his wife Sita, who was kidnapped by a demon king."

"And that one?" said Maya, pointing at a statue that was part man, part ape.

"Hmmm," mused *Naniamma*, peering past the priests in loincloths chanting over worshippers. "Yes, yes, that's Lord Hanuman—he helped free Sita."

"This is Ram Temple," said Zara, reading the sign hanging farther down.

"It's here," said Maya, pointing to where the temple was listed on the map. She drew a strong green line from the temple to Sunehri Mosque.

"Good job, girls," said *Naniamma*. "I don't know how I would have done this without you."

The girls glanced at each other, momentarily taken aback. Realization dawned that somehow, it seemed predestined that they come together. Each had a role to play in finding *Naniamma*'s treasure.

"Let's go," said Zara, giving Maya the nod to navigate.

Through a maze of narrow, congested lanes, they walked until they stumbled upon a small shop surrounded by a crowd of people, all watching a big-bellied cook who faced a huge pan filled with bubbling oil.

Naniamma stopped in her tracks, a childlike smile spreading across her face. "It's still here," she whispered reverently.

"What is it?" asked Zara, peering down at the map.

"It's Ghantewala," said *Naniamma*.

"A sweet shop?" said Maya, catching sight of the blue-and-yellow sign.

Naniamma nodded. "My father used to bring us here for *jalebis.*"

They joined the crush, watching the cook squeeze squiggles of batter from a muslin cloth bag into the hot oil, hands moving in quick circles. *They look like funnel cakes,* Maya thought. She'd eaten them in Karachi but had never seen them being made. Once golden brown, they were tossed in a vat of sugar syrup.

"Do you want one?" asked *Naniamma.*

At their eager nods, she purchased three and handed them out. Maya sank her teeth into the crisp surface, releasing warm, gooey sweetness. She closed her eyes with pleasure.

"It's still delicious," sighed *Naniamma.* "Three hundred years ago, the emperor's elephants would stop here and wouldn't budge until they got their treats!"

"This store has been here that long?" said Maya in wonder.

"Wow," added Zara, grinning at Maya before taking another bite. "I can't say I blame them."

Maya looked back at the map. Still eating, they paused in the shade of a tall, Gothic-style sandstone pillar, capped by a crucifix. As Maya probed the map for a detour, her sister read out the plaque at the pillar's base:

> *In memory of the officers and soldiers,*
> *British and native, of the Delhi Field Force*
> *who were killed in action or died of wounds*
> *or disease between the 30th May and 20th*
> *September 1857 . . .*

"What's this?" asked Zara.

Maya paused and matched the landmark to the page in their guidebook. "It's the Delhi Mutiny Memorial."

Naniamma grimaced. "Yes," she murmured. "Indian soldiers rose up in mutiny against the British. They wanted to restore the last Mughal emperor, Bahadur Shah Zafar, to power. So the British invaded Delhi in response. They razed much of the city and exiled the emperor and his family to Rangoon. The people of Delhi, both rich and poor, were evicted from their homes and massacred."

Zara inched away from the pillar, frowning.

"We'll go this way," said Maya, pointing down at the map.

They entered an alley where gold and silver jewelry

sparkled from shopwindows. A few blocks down, they slipped into a narrower alley, barely two feet wide. Zara took a left turn into a wider passage and they stumbled into a sprawling market that seemed to go on for a mile.

"Wow," muttered Maya, transfixed by the sight.

Embroidered silks, delicate lawns, rich velvets, heavy brocades, dyed cottons, soft wools, stiff linens, airy chiffons, jeweled taffetas, sparkling sequins, and delicate lace extended in all directions. Spools of fabric were stacked by color. There was an entire section of pink, from the palest blush to eye-jarring fuchsia—and so many shades of red, orange, yellow, green, violet, indigo, brown, white, and black that it would take years to figure out the range of hues. It reminded Maya of a similar place in Karachi, where her mother and aunts went to buy fabrics to take to their tailor. But nothing compared to the scale of this place.

"Incredible, isn't it?" said *Naniamma*.

As they reached the other end of the bazaar, *Naniamma* pointed in excitement. "There!" she said. Maya looked and spotted a glimmer of gold in the distance.

They emerged a block down from the mosque, a delicate building with a faded golden dome, overshadowed by the newer, clunky additions. Barely glancing at the building, *Naniamma* ran on, past old, decaying mansions.

"Naughara Lane, it should be here," muttered *Naniamma*, stopping at the third street. She froze, staring at a large house on the corner. "This is my uncle's house," she said, her voice hoarse, filled with excitement. She walked to the house next door and stood shaking at the crumbling steps.

The girls followed her up to a faded and scarred set of double doors, where their grandmother took a deep breath and knocked. When no one answered, she thumped again. Finally, they heard feet running up from the other side of the door.

"Who is it?" came a child's voice, speaking Hindi.

"I'm looking for the family of Mir Hayat," responded *Naniamma*.

There was silence.

"Please open the door," said *Naniamma*.

The door creaked open, and a small boy stood at the entrance. Maya peered over his head and glimpsed a vaulted passageway that led to a dusty courtyard.

"Salaam Alaikum," said *Naniamma*. "Is your mother here?"

The little boy frowned and looked at them

suspiciously. Then he pivoted and ran back through the open-air veranda and disappeared into the house. As Maya eyed the lone, stunted tree growing in the middle of the courtyard, the boy came back, a woman trailing him, dressed in a faded cotton sari, and with a red *bindi* marking her forehead, the sign of a married Hindu woman.

"What do you want?" she asked, approaching the door with a frown.

"I am looking for Mir Hayat's family," said *Naniamma*, her voice a little uncertain.

The woman shrugged. "There is no one here by that name."

"Are you sure?" asked *Naniamma*.

"Yes, yes. We've had this house for over twenty years," said the woman, her tone brusque. "My father-in-law bought it from an old man."

"The old man, where is he now?" asked *Naniamma*.

"Gone," said the woman. "I can't help you." Then she shut the door.

"This is not good," said Zara, a frown settling over her brow.

"But Mir Hayat said they would never move," said *Naniamma*.

7

Days Long Gone

Two hours later, after meandering through the back streets of Old Delhi, they finally stumbled upon what they were looking for: a storefront with a dusty green awning. After getting the door to Mir Hayat's old house shut in their faces, they'd stood on the steps, bitterly disappointed. *Naniamma*, pale and exhausted, had been about to say something, when they heard guttural singing from down the street.

"Come, examine my lovely, plump eggplants and sensational squash," warbled a grizzled old man, pushing a wooden cart piled with vegetables. "My tomatoes are incomparable and my okra divine!"

A hopeful smile lighting her face, *Naniamma* hurried down the steps—it was a known fact back in Karachi that vendors knew all the local gossip, since they came through the neighborhood every day. As *Naniamma* purchased a bag of limes from the man, she asked what had happened to the Hayat family. With a sigh, he told them that they had to move after their business fell on hard times. Although he didn't know where, he knew they still ran their bookshop in Urdu Bazaar, near Jama Mosque.

Maya found Urdu Bazaar on the map and off they went, passing yet another crumbling mansion, encircled by a protective metal gate. "This one's listed on the map," she said. "Haksar Haveli, where Nehru, the first prime minister of India, got married."

"Yes," said *Naniamma*, recollection animating her weary features. "Nehru's daughter, Indira Gandhi, became the second woman to rule India, after Razia Sultana. And when the Pakistani president came to Delhi for peace talks, he passed by here on the way to the house where he'd been born."

"The president of Pakistan was born in India?" asked Zara, surprised.

"Yes, his family left Delhi after Partition when he was a baby. He came back for the first time with his mother."

Maya gazed at the forlorn building with a pang of sadness. It had been a critical part of India's history and now it was just another ruin, home to wandering goats rummaging through the rubbish. The girls and their grandmother traveled east, past sizzling kebab stalls, a shop specializing in birds—homing pigeons, partridges, and songbirds—and a warehouse crammed with fireworks. A group of kids paid for a bagful and ran off, whispering and giggling with excitement.

"What are these used for?" Maya pondered out loud.

"They are set off during religious celebrations," explained *Naniamma*. "There is Muslim Eid, Zoroastrian New Year, Christmas, and the many Hindu holidays."

"Kids must be off from school for vacation all the time," said Maya, as they encountered a stall of garland makers preparing flower necklaces that brides and grooms wore at their weddings. *Nanabba should be here with us,* she thought glumly, trying not to trample the stray rose petals littering the ground.

"We're nearly there," said Zara, turning onto a quiet street. A jumble of bookshops lined both sides, including the one they were seeking. It was located beside Rizwan Book Depot. The crooked sign in

Urdu, Hindi, and English, announced: HAYAT'S BOOK-
SHOP AND HOUSE OF CALLIGRAPHY. Past the cracked
glass Maya spotted a wizened old man in a crisp white
kurta pyjama hunched over a desk, running his hand
through his silky white beard as he read a newspaper.
On either side of him stretched rickety bookshelves
crammed with books, manuscripts, and journals.

"This is it," whispered *Naniamma*, pausing to
smooth her sari before entering.

"Can I help you?" asked the old man eagerly,
folding away the paper. "I have rare tomes that may
interest you: poetry by Faiz or Ghalib, newly printed
novels—*Umrao Jan Ada*. Or I can prepare a letter in
Urdu if you need."

"Uh, no, thank you," said *Naniamma* nervously.
"I'm looking for Mir Hayat's family."

"Eh, speak up; I don't hear so well anymore," he
said, cupping his ear.

"I'm looking for Mir Hayat's family," *Naniamma*
repeated louder.

"Oh," he said. "I am Mir Hayat's youngest son,
Tariq."

"Tariq *Sahib*," said *Naniamma*, cheeks flushed with
relief and excitement. "I'm so pleased to meet you.
My father was Rayyan Mohammad Tauheed. His

brother, Hamza, had a house next to your father's."

Recognition sparkled in the man's cloudy gray eyes. "Oh, yes, my brothers and I played with his sons as children—stickball in the streets! I remember one of the boys—I think his name was Firaz—got us to steal *jalebis* from a sweet shop down the street. We got caught and were in so much trouble." He chuckled. "And your father—he used to come over for dinner whenever he was in town."

"Yes," said *Naniamma*, smiling. "My name is Alia, and sometimes my sisters and I would accompany him to Delhi from Aminpur."

"Yes," said Tariq *Sahib*. "I remember the fancy parties your uncle threw in your father's honor."

Naniamma nodded, relieved that he remembered.

"But I recall that your family moved to Pakistan," said Tariq *Sahib*. "Whatever became of them?"

Naniamma's face tightened. "They didn't survive the train passage."

Tariq *Sahib* took a ragged breath, additional creases weighing down his wrinkled cheeks. "'Surely we belong to Allah and to Him shall we return,'" he recited. "My heart aches at the news. Of course we heard such tales of horror—of trains arriving from Pakistan filled with murdered Hindus and Sikhs;

of cabins filled with slaughtered Muslims reaching Pakistan."

"Only I and two others survived," said *Naniamma*. "Ever since that day, I prayed that I would return. And here I am."

"It is a miracle you lived, my dear," said Tariq *Sahib*. "I'm so happy that you've returned to breathe the air and touch the soil where your family originated. At the stroke of midnight on the day of Partition, our family went into hiding, taken in by Hindu friends who protected us. For months the city burned and the people went mad. When we emerged, hardly any of the old inhabitants were left. Outsiders had taken over. Even our language was dead."

"How can a language die?" blurted Maya.

He waved his hand around his cramped shop. "Urdu, the language associated with Muslims, became an enemy, and was slowly purged from public life."

"But Urdu is still spoken here," said Maya, confused.

Tariq *Sahib* wrinkled his great long nose. "Urdu is an aristocratic language—the language of the poets. Now all that is left is its shabby ghost," he lamented. "People no longer have the knowledge of the *tehzeeb*, or culture, of the once glorious Delhi. Old Delhi is gone. . . . It's all gone, and those who were left behind are in misery, and those who were uprooted are in misery."

"That's terrible," said *Naniamma*.

Maya stood behind *Naniamma*, saddened by the anguish in the old man's face.

"But it's not just that," he continued. "Partition has left its poison in the blood of the people. Every other day there is terrible news of Muslims, Hindus, and Sikhs turning on one another. Just a few years ago, in the city of Ayodhya, an old mosque was torn down by Hindus claiming it had been built over their god Ram's temple. In the ensuing violence, thousands were killed."

Killed. The word ricocheted through Maya's mind.

"We read about the riots in the newspaper," said *Naniamma*. "It's a shame that the damage done at Partition continues to this day. Even in Pakistan, created to protect the interests of Muslims, there is corruption and unrest among the different ethnic and religious groups—the rich become richer while the rest wallow in poverty, without proper health care or education."

In the silence that followed, Zara gently tugged on *Naniamma*'s arm. "The keys . . . ," she whispered.

"Oh, yes," said *Naniamma*. "Tariq *Sahib*, my father

left the keys and the deed to our house with your father. Do you have them?"

Tariq *Sahib* paused to think, stroking his beard. "I do recall some such things." He looked up, eyes brightening with remembrance. "Before my father passed away, he told my brothers and me about your father and uncle. And showed us a sealed package, telling us to give it to them if they returned."

"Do you still have it?" asked *Naniamma* eagerly.

"They should be in my father's old suitcase," he said. "Let me go to our apartment upstairs and check."

He returned a few minutes later. "These are the items that your family left in my father's care," he said.

"Thank you so much for keeping them safe," said *Naniamma* as she stared at the frayed velvet pouch in his hands.

"Of course, of course," said Tariq *Sahib*. He loosened the strings of the pouch and turned the contents over into her open hands: a jumble of iron keys and a yellowed bundle of papers.

Naniamma stroked the largest key, engraved with a series of numbers in Urdu. "This is for our house in Aminpur."

Tariq *Sahib* sadly shook his head. "Although the deed and key prove ownership, it will be very difficult to claim your house. Even if you do, you'll have a nightmare of a time trying to legally evict those who've moved in."

"I see," said *Naniamma*, placing everything back in the bag.

"You must stay for dinner and meet my wife," said Tariq *Sahib*.

"Thank you so much for the invitation," said *Naniamma* gently, "but we need to prepare for our trip to Aminpur. Perhaps on our return we can stop by for tea."

"As you wish," said Tariq *Sahib*, taking a slim volume from a shelf. "Sadly, this India is not the one you left, but best of luck on your journey. Please accept this as a token of my respect and admiration."

"Thank you," said *Naniamma*, taking the book. On its cover was a bearded man.

"That is Mirza Ghalib, the court poet to Bahadur Shah, the last Mughal emperor," said Tariq *Sahib*. "My favorite poem is 'Temple Lamps.' Be sure to read it."

With that they parted, but Tariq *Sahib*'s words echoed in Maya's mind: *Old Delhi is gone. . . . It's all gone, and those who were left behind are in misery, and those who were uprooted are in misery.* As they exited, she felt a rumble in her belly.

"How about we eat something before heading back to the hotel?" suggested *Naniamma*.

"Great idea," said Zara. "Where should we go?"

"Check the book," said *Naniamma*, glancing at Maya. "It's led us in the right direction so far."

Maya located a place nearby, Karim's: a restaurant "fit for kings—literally," said the guidebook, as it was owned by the descendants of royal Mughal cooks. They walked past the bustling open-air kitchen, where men danced in an age-old ballet, some stirring huge stainless steel pots while others grilled meat on flames and flattened disks of dough to be placed inside blistering clay ovens. The waiter seated them at a table and handed them menus.

"It's like Bundoo Khan," muttered Maya, remembering the restaurant in Karachi. She'd been hoping to find something she was familiar with. But it was *all* familiar. There were kebabs—chicken, lamb, and fish. *Parathas*—plain or stuffed with potatoes or minced meat. A dozen biryanis, royal rice dishes, and vegetable dishes—creamed spinach, peas, cauliflower, and lentils. It was like she was staring down at a menu in Pakistan.

"Even though they are now two countries, the recipes were formulated in the same kitchens before

1947," said *Naniamma*. "Bundoo Khan brought his recipes to Karachi from his hometown in India. Of course, there are regional differences," she added as the waiter placed a sizzling plate of kebabs in front of them. "The food in the South has its own unique flavors and ingredients."

As Maya took a *paratha* and added a piece of juicy boneless lamb kebab to her plate, *Naniamma* added absentmindedly, "And India has many vegetarians, since many Hindus, Jains, and Buddhists don't eat meat."

After the waiter left, *Naniamma* quieted, lost in her own thoughts. Maya noticed that her grandmother's hand shook as she reached to take a piece of flaky *paratha*, and she worried that the day had taken a toll on her. A long journey lay ahead of them. She needed to get back to the hotel and get some rest.

A deep, sweet weariness in her bones, Maya grabbed her journal and settled into the bed to log the day's events while *Naniamma* and Zara bustled about, preparing for their trip the next day. She pulled out her colored pencils and drew a map of Old Delhi marked with the locations they'd traveled to that day.

• • •

Saturday, September 17, continued.
New Delhi, India

India is not how I imagined it would be.
I was expecting it to feel unfamiliar, but
everything we saw reminded me of Pakistan:
the people, the eggplant and okra in the market,
the beggars on the street, the monsoon rains,
rickshaws, sticky, sweet jalebis, and the shaggy
white goats roaming the streets. And in both
Delhi and Karachi, there are places that are
very beautiful and places that are very sad.

Tomorrow we will take the train to Faizabad.
We're leaving later than we'd like, though,
because of Navaratri, the Hindu festival
symbolizing the triumph of good over evil. Want
to know the other name for Navaratri? It's
Durga Puja. Remember I mentioned that Durga
is another name for Maya? How weird is that?
Since the festival starts in the morning, the
trains are full. The only availability was on the
overnight sleeper. We're staying at a hotel in
Faizabad, then taking a car to Aminpur. If
things go according to plan, we'll find the chest
and return to Delhi the day after tomorrow.

. . .

As she turned to put her journal on the side table, Maya spotted the book Tariq *Sahib* had given her grandmother. She picked it up and began flipping through the pages. "Listen to this," she said. "It's the poem Tariq *Sahib* mentioned, by Ghalib."

"We don't have time for poetry," grumbled Zara, digging through her backpack.

"No, no, go ahead and read some of it," said *Nani-amma*.

So Maya cleared her throat and began.

> *"Father and son are at each other's throat;*
> *Brother fights brother. Unity*
> *And Federation are undermined.*
> *Despite all these ominous signs*
> *Why has not doomsday come?*
> *Why does not the Last Trumpet sound?*
> *Who holds the reins of the final catastrophe?"*
> *The hoary old man of lucent ken*
> *Pointed toward Kashi and gently smiled.*
> *"The Architect," he said, "is fond of this edifice*
> *Because of which there is colour in life; He*
> *would not like it to perish and fall."*

"What does it mean?" asked Maya.

Naniamma paused from folding a sari. "Ghalib lived during the time when the Moghuls lost power to the British," she said. "What do *you* think he's saying?"

Zara stood, a thoughtful look on her face. She had been listening despite her grumbling. "The British used divide and conquer to pit everyone against each other," she said. "So when Ghalib saw how bad the fighting was, he wondered why the end hadn't come."

Naniamma nodded, looking pleased. "But 'the architect' wouldn't let it fall apart."

"The architect is God, isn't it?" asked Zara.

"Yes," said *Naniamma*.

"And because of him, the architect, there is color in life," she added.

"Correct," replied *Naniamma*. "Now, let's get to bed. It's going to be a busy day tomorrow."

Maya put away the book. It seemed to her that the poem prophesized the pain and conflict Partition would one day bring. With that thought she fell into a deep sleep.

Maya was cold. Groggily, she opened her eyes and saw that the bathroom light was on and the door was wide open. *Something's not right.* She sat up suddenly and glanced around the room. On the floor lay *Nani-amma*'s crumpled form.

Her breath seizing in her throat, Maya slid out of bed. *"Naniamma!"* she cried, crouching beside her.

There was no response. Maya grabbed her grand-mother's icy hands and pressed her cheek against her chest. There was a faint heartbeat, like a small bird fluttering in a cage. "Zara," she yelled toward the other bed, "wake up . . . something's wrong!"

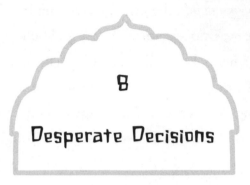

8

Desperate Decisions

"WHERE ARE YOUR PARENTS?" asked Dr. Kumar, a frown causing the red *bindi* on her forehead to scrunch up.

The sisters stared at the doctor, a willowy woman in a white coat, wondering what to say. Maya looked at *Naniamma*, who lay asleep, a tiny form huddled under the white sheets of the hospital bed.

"They aren't here . . . ," began Zara, her voice hoarse. "We were traveling with our grandmother and just arrived in Delhi."

"Oh," said Dr. Kumar, comprehension settling over her fine, dark features as she reviewed the medical charts. "Well, it looks like your grandmother had a stroke."

"A stroke?" squawked Zara, as Maya's pulse raced. "Is she going to be okay?"

"Well, her blood pressure was highly elevated when she came in. Does she have a heart condition?"

"Yes," whispered Maya. "She forgot her medicine at home."

"Uncontrolled blood pressure can disrupt blood supply to the brain," explained Dr. Kumar, her face sympathetic. "But luckily it was a minor stroke and we caught it in time. So although she's weak and needs time to recover, she's stable and there doesn't seem to be permanent damage."

"Oh, thank God," said Zara, reaching over to grip Maya's hand.

"Where are you coming from, then?" asked Dr. Kumar, snapping the file shut.

"From Karachi," mumbled Zara.

"Pakistan?" Dr. Kumar raised her her eyebrows.

"Uh, yes," replied Zara.

"Well, you need to call your parents right away and have them come to Delhi," she said. "Arrangements need to be made for your grandmother's care—she may have to stay in the hospital a few more days, then she'll need help flying home. I think it's best if you call them from my office so your grandmother can have some peace and quiet. Also, I'd like to talk to them as well."

Maya watched the doctor's long black braid sway with her brisk pace as she followed her down the hall. Images from the last three hours flashed through her mind: Zara crying, shouting into the telephone . . . hotel staff rushing to the room . . . the ambulance ride through Delhi at three in the morning . . . her grandmother disappearing into an examining room while the sisters waited nervously on hard waiting room chairs.

"Hello," Zara whispered into her bright pink cell phone.

"Zara, is that you?" shrieked Sofia *Khala*. Maya, sitting beside her sister, heard every muffled word. "Are you okay? We've been *frantic* with worry." Before Zara could respond, Maya heard her aunt shouting. "Someone, go get Dalia, it's Zara," bellowed Sofia *Khala*.

"Zara?" came their mother's voice from another line. "What were you girls thinking, running off like that?"

"I was just . . . ," said Zara, but her mother cut her off.

"Give the phone to your grandmother. I need to talk to her," said their mother.

"Mom," said Zara. "*Naniamma* is sick."

A pause followed. "What do you mean, she's sick?"

"She had a stroke. . . . A *minor* stroke."

"*What?*" she gasped. "When did that happen?"

"Last night, at the hotel," explained Zara. "We're at a hospital now."

"How is she?" cried her mother.

"Doing much better," said Zara in a rush. "The doctor says she's in stable condition, and she's asleep."

"Well, you stay put," said her mother. "I'm coming there on the next flight, do you understand?"

"Yes," replied Zara.

"Is the doctor there?" asked her mother.

"Yes, I'm in her office," said Zara.

"Give her the phone."

Zara handed the phone to Dr. Kumar, who sat on the other side of the smooth wooden desk, "She's not awake yet. . . . I've given her a mild sedative to help her sleep. . . . She cannot be moved for a few days; she is too weak and needs to recover. . . . Yes, I urge you or someone in your family to come at once."

"Water," came a feeble request.

Maya's eyes snapped open. The sisters had fallen

asleep in the lumpy chairs beside the hospital bed, and now it was late in the afternoon.

"Water."

Still groggy, Maya jumped up to grab a glass from the side table and poured water from a jug. "Here you go, *Naniamma*," she said, relieved that she was awake.

"Thanks, *jaan*," said *Naniamma*. After a long gulp, she lay back with a sigh. "What happened? Where are we?" she asked, peering over the sheets.

"You had a stroke, a ministroke," explained Zara, rushing over, eyes bleary. "Your blood pressure shot up and you collapsed because you weren't taking your medication."

"We're at a hospital," added Maya.

"But we have to go," said *Naniamma*, confused. "We have a train to catch."

"*Naniamma* . . . ," said Zara, trying to find the words. "You can't go—you're too sick."

"But I've come this far," said *Naniamma*, blinking rapidly, groggy from the drugs. "I must go—" She sat up and swung her legs over the side of the bed. She tried to take a step. Zara and Maya caught her right as her knees buckled under her. As gently as they could, they guided her back into bed.

"Why is this happening?" whispered *Naniamma* as

the sisters settled her under the blanket. "It took over forty years but I came . . . to find the chest . . . get Malik's ring . . . see my mother's face again. . . ."

Malik . . . *Nanabba.* Maya remembered his body wrapped in sheets, waiting to be buried with the promised engagement ring. Warring emotions raced through her: deep sadness coupled with red hot anger. It wasn't fair. They'd come so far.

"It's over before it even began," whispered *Nani-amma* as tears ran down the sides of her face.

"Naniamma," whispered Zara. "It will be okay. . . ."

"No . . . ," came her defeated response. "Despite all the hope and planning . . . it's over. . . ."

"No!" cried Zara, two angry spots of color on her cheeks. "Don't say that."

Maya took her grandmother's hand, watching her strained features. *Naniamma* was stubborn even in defeat, as she struggled to keep from falling into a drugged sleep. As she faded, she squeezed Maya's fingers and looked from one sister to the other. "So many promises. . . . My promise to find the chest . . . Malik's to bring me here . . . All broken . . ." Exhaling, *Naniamma* went limp, falling into the deep, dark well of the drug's effects.

Zara slowly turned to face Maya, her face streaked

with tears. "We also promised that we would help her," she whispered.

Maya nodded, painful words caught in her throat in a hard lump.

Then her sister got that look on her face—the bullheaded-rhino look. She looked down at her watch, glanced at Maya, and smiled.

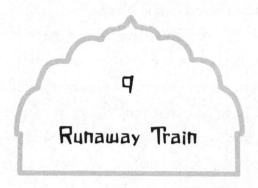

9

Runaway Train

"ARE YOU *SURE* THIS is a good idea?" Maya asked again, twisting her hands as Zara propped a hastily written note for their mother against the water jug.

"Look," said Zara, "don't worry so much. We traveled all the way to Little Rock last year to visit Sofia *Khala* by ourselves. It was easy."

Maya remembered. They'd changed planes in Houston without a problem.

"It'll be fine," urged her sister. "We need to hurry if we're going to make the train."

Maya considered her sister's argument. *Naniamma had* made all the arrangements—train tickets, hotel, and car service in Faizabad. All they had to do was follow the memory map to the house in Aminpur. "But what if the chest isn't there?" she asked pragmatically, hating to make rushed decisions.

"Look, we've come this far, we have to see this through," said Zara impatiently. "What if it is there—can you imagine how happy *Naniamma* will be?"

Maya imagined presenting the chest to their grandmother. She would be overjoyed. And *Nanabba*, he'd get his ring. "Okay," she exhaled. "We owe it to her to help finish what we started together."

"Good." Zara smiled and hurried toward the door. "We'll be back the day after tomorrow, before Mom has time to get herself totally worked up."

Pushing aside the desire to give her grandmother a kiss, since she might wake her, Maya joined Zara just inside the doorway, scanning the hospital hallway to make sure none of the nurses or Dr. Kumar was around. Coast clear, they exited their grandmother's room and found a taxi.

At the hotel they packed quickly, tossing their clothes into a shared backpack. As Zara rifled through her grandmother's handbag for money—Indian rupees and hundred-dollar bills—tucking them into her

small purse along with her cell phone, Maya spotted *Naniamma*'s memory map on the side table. Gently folding it in half, she slid it into the guidebook
and stuck the book into the backpack along with
her journal and the train tickets. Zara added their
passports, the iron key to their great-grandfather's
house, and the confirmation document for Maurya
Hotel, hiding them all in an inside pocket.

As Maya watched her sister zip up her purse, she
paused, stomach suddenly in knots. "You know Mom's
going to be way beyond bubbling-volcano mad when
she finds us missing, don't you? She's going to ground
us for a year," she added, trying to find a chink in her
sister's resolve.

"Look," said Zara, pausing a moment, face soften-
ing as if she finally realized Maya's fear. "We can do
this—how hard can it be?"

The resistance Maya felt nearly melted, though a
tiny bit remained. Her sister was right—*Naniamma*
had already planned out the trip, step by step.

"Okay, then," said Zara, taking the backpack.
"Let's go."

The girls rode the elevator down to the lobby in
silence, and as they neared the exit, they ran into Cyrus,
the manager, heading toward the doors, briefcase in

hand. His sea-green eyes brightened when he spotted them. "How is your grandmother?"

Zara slowed, not wanting to waste time or answer too many nosy questions. "She's awake, doing much better, thanks."

"Well, if you need anything, please let us know. Ms. Gupta will be taking over my post and she can help in any way you need." He pointed to a young woman in a gray suit and bright red lipstick greeting guests.

"Can you arrange for a taxi to take us back to the . . . hospital?" asked Zara.

"Certainly," Cyrus said, stepping toward the line of hotel-managed taxis. "Gopi," he called out to a driver standing near a shiny white car. "Please take Miss Zara and Miss Maya to Apollo Hospital." As they climbed inside, Cyrus paused. "I can accompany you if you wish, for any assistance."

Maya froze. Oh, no . . .

"Oh, but it's not necessary," Zara blurted out.

"Have a safe journey and give my best wishes to your grandmother," said Cyrus.

"We will," said Zara as she pulled the door shut. As the car pulled onto the road, she turned to the driver. "Gopi, Delhi Junction Station, quickly."

"But, miss," said the driver, confused. "Mr. Cyrus said to go to Apollo Hospital."

"There's been a change of plans," said Zara. Maya cringed at her imperious tone. "I need to meet . . . my father at the train station. He is coming in from Mumbai."

Gopi nodded, frowned, but didn't argue. He shrugged and merged back into traffic, which was snarled with commuters returning home.

Forty-five minutes later, they'd barely crawled more than a mile up the clogged road, penned in by a pack of scooters, cars, buses, rickshaws, and donkey carts.

Maya glanced down at her watch: 6:23. The sun was low on the horizon and the train left in thirty-seven minutes. Panic bloomed in her chest. "We're not going to make it to the train station on time," she whispered to her sister.

Zara nodded, frowning. "Can't we go any faster?" she asked Gopi, who sat fiddling with the CD, playing hip-gyrating Bollywood hits.

"Miss, this is Delhi traffic." He shrugged. "The station is only a few minutes away—the next left, past Mahatma Gandhi Park."

The sisters peered through the windshield, examining a long stretch of yellow brick that lay the foundation of Town Hall, which was trimmed with carved white stone. An expansive park stretched behind.

"We can't miss the train," muttered Zara, jaw clenched as the car stopped yet again. To Maya's surprise, she pulled on the backpack, took out a handful of bills from her purse, and handed the rupees to Gopi. "Come on," she said, grabbing Maya's hand. She pushed open the door and jumped out.

Maneuvering past an idling city bus belching exhaust, they leapt onto the sidewalk facing a cinema. Bollywood movie posters announced the latest hits; swashbuckling heroes, with the last name of Khan, posed in tight jeans and leather jackets or snazzy suits, sharing steamy looks with long-lashed heroines in sequins. Zara sprinted past Town Hall, pulling Maya behind her. They ran past a bronze statue of Gandhi, a perch for dozing pigeons.

Over the treetops Maya glimpsed red turrets rising up in an ominous violet sky. The color heralded secrecy and sometimes cruelty. Maya gulped, following her sister along the crosswalk through the main gates of Delhi Junction Station. They circumvented vendors balancing trays of candy, and shoe polishers clapping brushes to attract customers.

6:48. *Twelve minutes to find the right platform,* thought Maya, following Zara up the steps toward the entryway, where a man in a flowered polyester shirt lounged.

"Let me help you, miss," he called to Zara, smiling beneath a lush mustache.

Naniamma's voice rang in Maya's head. *Ignore anyone who tries to sell you something or tries to offer help.*

"No, thanks," said Zara, clearly remembering the warning too, and she strode past to enter the station. Inside, she paused as a red-uniformed porter loaded with heavy suitcases crossed their path. A portly woman in a flowing mustard-and-orange sari sailed by, herding three teenage girls, all clutching their purses. Zara tightened her grip on the backpack as they stared out over the bustling Delhi Junction concourse. The immense station sprawled out in front of them, a sea of iridescent colors, swimming with travelers, hawkers, beggars, and, she was certain, pickpockets. Maya gulped, ears bombarded with the cacophony of a thousand voices, coupled with blaring music and rumbling trains. The noise dulled the buzzing of the loudspeaker, which was informing passengers of arriving trains, changed platforms, and delays.

"Where do we go?" said Maya, clutching Zara's arm.

"Hold on," replied Zara, peering along the con-course. "We need to find a train schedule that can direct us to the right platform."

"Excuse us," interrupted a tired, Australian-accented voice behind them. Zara pulled Maya aside to let a troop of disheveled backpackers pass.

"Let's find our train, mate," said the wiry guy in the lead, running a hand through shaggy blond locks. "The platforms change all the time and I don't want to miss it."

"But I'm famished, man," grumbled a stocky guy beside him, tugging at his sweat-soaked T-shirt.

"We'll look for some nosh after," said the blond.

"Be careful this time," piped up a deep voice from the back. "My stomach was raging for days after we ate that flaming chicken *vindaloo* at the Goa station, man."

"Remember what the bloke at the hotel said," reminded the blond, snorting with laughter. "Only eat things that are hot and just out of the pot. No sal-ads, no unbottled water . . ."

Sharing a grin, the sisters scurried after them to an electronic display board. There it was: the Delhi-Faizabad Express, leaving from platform 6.

"We only have five minutes till it arrives," said Zara, grabbing Maya's hand. "Come on!"

As they hurried on, a whirring sounded from the board.

"Hey," said Maya, craning her neck back. "Can we just check the number again?"

"We know already!" cried Zara, circumventing a *chaiwallah*, a tea vendor. "Do you want to miss the train?"

Maya swallowed a retort and followed, though she wished she'd gotten a confirming look. They ran through the concourse toward a set of stairs to the second level, where pathways crisscrossed above the tracks. At the top step Maya paused, blinking in confusion. The platforms were not in numerical order. Platforms 2, 5, and 8 were to the right, toward the east wing of the station. Arrows directed passengers west toward 3, 7, and 9.

Maya glanced from one direction to the other. *Six, where's six?* People pushed past them, hauling cumbersome bundles and suitcases. She peered over the balcony and as she looked for a sign for 6, her eyes wavered. Hidden away, almost invisible, were packs of kids—tucked in the shadows, scampering across the tracks. *That looks dangerous. Where are their parents?* Then it hit her—they were street children. A piteous little girl sat in front of a beggar's bowl, her arm missing. A sickening feeling settled in Maya's gut. She glanced back to Zara, who was talking to a man in a crisp khaki uniform. He was slurping a cup of tea and twirling a baton. *A policeman!*

"You must be going the other way," he said, pointing with his baton. "It is the second-to-last stairs."

"Thank you," said Zara.

Grabbing Maya's hand, she took off as the speakers crackled to life, spewing out unintelligible announcements. At the second-to-last set of stairs, a stretch of crimson metal pulled into the platform. The word "danger" popped into Maya's head as she stared at the passenger cars, swarmed by a mass of people clambering aboard.

"Come on!" cried Zara, yanking her down the steps just as the train's whistle blew, giving them scant minutes to board.

An image of a blood-soaked train compartment appeared from *Naniamma*'s story and Maya hesitated, but her sister pulled her toward the first passenger car. Maya glanced down at her ticket. The concierge had booked first-class air-conditioned compartments for them since their grandmother had wanted to have a private room with beds and a lockable door. The train car that stood in front of them read: "second class." "This is the wrong section!" she cried.

"Don't worry about that now," said Zara, pushing Maya ahead of her. "We just need to get on."

Ducking past flying elbows and bulky packages, Maya grabbed the metal rail and hauled herself up the steps onto the train. She squeezed past harried passengers and went up the cramped corridor, which extended the length of the car and was lined with windows on the left. On the right were compartments fitted with wooden benches facing each other, a bunk on top. All were full, but at the third one Maya spotted a bare spot on the floor, beneath the window. The rest of the space was taken up by an elderly couple traveling with a young woman and six children. When the old woman spotted the girls, she smiled and waved them inside.

"Go, hurry," urged Zara, pushing Maya inside.

Maya climbed over luggage and prepared to sit down, her sister squeezing in beside her. Before she sat, she lay her jean jacket on the grimy floor. She'd just secured the backpack in her lap when the whistle blew and the train pulled away from the station.

"We did it," Zara laughed giddily, ruffling Maya's hair.

"Yeah," replied Maya, a niggling feeling of doubt lurking in the back of her mind.

"We'll get the chest and be back in no time," said Zara confidently.

Maya leaned back against the wall, feeling the wind whip her hair as it whooshed through the bars on the window.

Zara looked around the cramped but secure space. "Let's wait a bit till things settle down. It might be better to just get off at the next stop and make our way to the right compartment."

"Okay," said Maya. For once, she appreciated her sister's bullheadedness, though she would never admit it. *I'm glad we're doing this,* she thought. *Nanabba would have wanted us to.* She sighed, staring down at her ticket. A long journey lay before them, so she leaned over to retrieve her journal from their backpack.

"Hey, pass me my book, would you?" asked Zara.

"Sure," replied Maya, double-checking their passports, money, hotel reservation, and return tickets to Delhi before finding what she needed. Under the flickering light of the compartment, she cracked open the guidebook to a map and copied it into her journal, outlining the route from Delhi to Faizabad in black.

Sunday, September 18
Train from Delhi to Faizabad

Here are some facts about Indian railroads:

1. In 1844, the first proposal to construct a railroad in India was presented to the East India Company in London.

2. The total distance covered by the 14,300 trains of Indian Railways equals three and a half times the distance to the moon.

3. If the tracks of Indian Railways were to be laid out, they would circle the earth almost 1.5 times.

4. With over 1.6 million employees, Indian Railways is the world's 9th-largest employer.

5. The trains carry more than 25 million passengers every day, more than the entire population of Australia.

6. The station with the longest name is Venkatanarasimharajuvaripeta.

7. Indian Railways has a mascot—Bholu, the guard elephant.

Along with tea, the British brought the railway to India. It was a pretty smart thing to do since they could use it to connect the huge country and rule it more efficiently. Seventy years ago, my grandmother and her family were on a train like this one, headed to Pakistan. That trip didn't have a happy ending. Hopefully ours will.

Maya stared down at the last line with a frown, wondering if she should explain to her teacher that she and Zara had taken off on their own. Before she could even think how to put that into words, she was distracted as the elderly woman reached up to the top bunk. As the little kids crowded around her, she brought down a huge stacked, metal lunch box. The younger woman spread out a piece of cloth on top of a suitcase, then unlatched the three tiers of metal dishes and laid them out. Spicy fragrances spilled out into the compartment as the children jostled to get closer. The woman handed each a *roti*, whole-wheat flatbread, filled with a scoop of potatoes and peas. She turned to the sisters and pointed from them to the food with a warm smile. Maya eyed the bright green peas. She was not a fan of their squishy green centers, but the thought of her grandmother's comment of them being peas in a pod made her feel a bit more warmly toward the smooshy green vegetable.

"No, thank you," said Zara in her accented Urdu, smiling.

The warnings from the backpackers flared in Maya's mind and she politely shook her head too. They could not afford to get sick, no matter how good it looked. As the family enjoyed their meal, Maya sat watching the landscape beyond the window. All traces of the city had disappeared and it seemed as if they'd entered a different world. A stretch of lush farmland rolled along beside them, where women in bright skirts and shining bangles picked baskets of pale cauliflower. Past a field of corn, a group of children splashed in a pond, giving their docile blue-black water buffalo a good scrubbing. Maya returned their wave, watching them laugh and splash. Exhaustion tugging at her eyelids, she rested her head on Zara's shoulder. When she didn't get shoved away as she expected, she let her eyes drift shut, lulled by the sway of the train.

"Excusing me, miss." A gruff voice broke through her sleep.

Maya's eyelids flew open and she saw a stooped man in a dark blue jacket and cap standing at the door.

"Your ticket, please," he requested.

"Zara, wake up," Maya said groggily, shaking her sleeping sister, who woke up and handed over their tickets to the collector. He gazed down at them with a frown.

He's probably wondering why we're not in the right compartment, thought Maya. *Maybe he'll show us how to get to first class.* A bed and a lock in a private room sounded heavenly right now. They probably had another eight hours before they reached Faizabad and they could get a proper nap.

"Where are you going?" he asked, peering at her over his horn-rimmed glasses.

"Faizabad," replied Zara. "I know we're in the wrong compartment," she added.

The man blinked. "No, miss. You are on the *wrong train.*"

10

Misdirection

ALL TRACES OF SLEEP vanished in a flash as Maya stared at the attendant with wide eyes. Her sister gasped. "What do you mean, *wrong* train?"

"This is the Rajasthan Express to Jaipur."

Fear constricted Maya's insides. "Jaipur?" she squeaked.

"Is that on the way to Faizabad?" interrupted Zara, scrambling to stand up.

"No." He shook his head. "Faizabad is to the east. We are journeying south."

"Oh, no," said Zara, clutching her hands together as Maya rose beside her.

"I told you," said Maya, as angry indignation rose within her, alongside the fear. "I told you we should check the board again."

"Okay, okay, calm down," said Zara, looking panicked herself.

Maya snorted and turned to the conductor. "Sir, we need to go to Faizabad. . . . What do we do?"

"You must be off-loading at the next station," he said. "From there you will be needing to change tickets."

"Is the next stop coming up?" asked Zara, running a hand through her usually perfect bob, which was sticking out in places.

"Yes, arriving shortly," he replied as Maya glanced down at her watch, heart racing. It was 9:05. They'd been going the wrong way for two hours.

The conductor looked around the compartment quizzically, staring at the dozing family, then back at them. "Where are your companions? Mother, father? Aunty?"

"Oh," muttered Zara. "They're meeting us at the train station."

"In Faizabad?" he asked, giving her an odd look.

"Uh, yes," she said, straightening her back as Maya cringed at the lie.

"Miss," he said, eyes troubled, "after you are changing tickets, stay in the waiting room until the train arrives."

Zara nodded, shifting uncomfortably.

"But you need to be paying me for this portion of the travel," he said, pulling out a receipt booklet. Zara dug through her wallet for the fare and handed it to him. "Remember the waiting room," he repeated, then shuffled on.

"Come on," said Zara, giving Maya a reassuring but strained smile. "It'll be okay. We just got a little off track, that's all."

Maya bit her tongue. There was no point in arguing with Zara; it usually got her nowhere. Quickly gathering their things, the girls stepped over a sleeping little girl and exited the compartment, nodding to the grandmother, who gazed after them with curiosity.

"We'll wait by the doors," said Zara. "That way we can be the first to get off."

Maya ignored her and grabbed a spot beside a window overlooking a dark expanse stretching out beside them. There were no electric lights, just the pale illumination from the full moon above, displaying slumbering villages and fields. As she took in a deep, calming gulp of cool air, redolent with diesel and cut grass, she spotted a burst of lightning in the distance, indicating that clouds, bulging with monsoon rain, were not far off.

"Look," said Zara in a small voice. "I'm sorry, okay? This is totally my fault."

Maya looked at her sister in surprise. She didn't recall her ever apologizing, even when she was dead wrong. "It's okay," she replied, deciding to be magnanimous. They had a long journey ahead of them and it would be painful if they weren't talking to each other. "Let's just figure out how to get back on track to Faizabad."

Zara nodded, relieved. They stood touching shoulders as the train flew along a curve, approaching a metal bridge straddling a sinuous river. A city dotted with lights glimmered in the distance. As the train thundered across the bridge, something else caught Maya's eye, rising from the bank—a glowing beacon, its unmistakable dome shining like burnished silver in the moonlight.

"Look," she whispered, nudging Zara.

"It's . . . it's that building . . . the really famous one . . . Taj something," said Zara, distracted for a moment from the crisis at hand.

The girls stared in wonder as the building faded in

the distance and a whistle shrilled above, announcing their arrival. The sisters jumped from the train and made a beeline for the ticket booth. With just six platforms, Agra Cantt was a much more manageable station, but the crowds, even at night, were sizable. Zara gripped Maya's hand as they pushed past passengers, porters, hawkers, and a small boy in a frayed Mickey Mouse T-shirt sweeping the floor in front of the waiting room.

The kind ticket collector's words rang in Maya's ear as they passed: *Stay in the waiting room until your train arrives.*

Making a mental note to return to the waiting room, she allowed Zara to steer her toward the long line in front of the ticket window.

"Give me my passport," said Zara as they reached the front of the line. "I'll need identification to purchase the tickets."

As Maya extracted her sister's passport from the inside pocket of the backpack, a few hundred-dollar bills dislodged and fell.

"Be careful," whispered Zara, scooping them up. She grabbed the passport and turned to the counter, leaving Maya to nervously gaze at the passengers in line behind them.

"Our train leaves in two hours," said Zara a few

minutes later, looking relieved. "I had to use up most of the Indian money, but we have dollars left."

"That's great," said Maya, clutching the backpack.

"Yeah, we'll be in Faizabad by nine tomorrow," said Zara.

Maya followed Zara back toward the waiting room, but the smell of frying bread and simmering curry made them slow. Tucked away to the right was a line of food vendors, where a cheery-faced woman had just placed a bowl of boiled eggs on her counter beside a stack of *parathas*.

"I think the last time we ate was at Karim's," said Zara, eyeing a vendor spoon rice into bowls and top it with a peppery chicken stew.

Maya's mouth watered. "I'm starving."

"Okay, let's get something to eat," said Zara.

"Wait," said Maya. "Nothing raw or lukewarm."

They purchased half a dozen sealed packages of cookies, bottles of water, and bananas. A real meal would have to wait for the hotel. As they turned toward the waiting room, the boy in the Mickey Mouse T-shirt appeared beside them, a thoughtful look on his lean, smudged face. With matted curly hair, a dimpled chin, and scarred knees, he couldn't have been older than nine.

He looks hungry. Probably one of the dozens of homeless kids roaming the station, she thought, looking for a way to earn a few rupees. She handed him a packet of cookies and patted him on the shoulder with a smile. He looked surprised.

"We should go to the bathroom," said Zara.

"I don't need to," said Maya, imagining the restrooms and wrinkling her nose.

"Okay," said Zara, holding up a finger and waving it as if she were a disobedient puppy. "Stay here and don't move."

"Yeah, yeah . . . I know," muttered Maya, standing with the bag slung over her shoulder. As she peeled a banana, she felt a sharp tug on her backpack. Surprised, she turned, losing her balance at another insistent yank. Before she could regain her footing, a third, more forceful jerk dropped her to the ground. She looked up to see a boy racing toward the main exit, dragging her backpack behind him.

Stunned, she lay speechless. "Thief," she finally croaked, leaping up. "Zara!" she yelled, pounding on the door of the bathroom.

"What?" came an irritated reply.

"The backpack . . . a kid stole the backpack!"

"What!" she screamed. "Hold on . . ."

The boy, the one in the Mickey Mouse T-shirt, Maya noticed, was quickly disappearing into the crowd.

We can't wait, thought Maya. Naniamma's *memory map is in there . . . the key to the house, our passports. . . .* She ran, weaving through the crowd, pausing to jump over a sleeping man. *Where is he?* She scanned the crowd desperately. Without thinking twice, she ran, shouting "Thief!" at the top of her lungs, but no one paid them much attention; it was as if they were invisible. The boy had nearly made it to the main gate and was about to slip through when Maya shouted again, frantically looking for a khaki uniform.

"Police . . . help!"

The boy looked back, eyes fearful as a man in a safari suit paused in midstride. Before the boy could slither past, he grabbed his T-shirt.

Relief filled Maya, weakening her bones. "He took my bag," she gasped, running toward them.

Just as she reached them, the boy dropped the bag and fell to his knees. As the man tried to hold on, the boy twisted, maneuvering his shirt over his head and arms. In a blink of an eye he slipped out, leaving the man holding his shirt, a look of surprise on his face. Backpack hanging off his bare back, the boy ran toward Maya. As she lunged for him, he pivoted left, running toward the last platform.

Maya scrambled after him but before she could make sense of which direction he was going, he leapt off the platform and onto the tracks. A deafening whistle reverberated through the air, announcing that a train was approaching. Blinded by the desire to get back the bag, Maya jumped onto the tracks, falling to her knees on jagged gravel. With a muffled curse, she got up and ran across the tracks, feeling the ground quake from the approach of metal wheels.

"Maya!" she heard Zara scream from the platform.

Maya glanced back and saw her sister waving frantically, trying to reach her. *The bag . . . I need to get the bag. . . .* She picked up speed and ran, gaining ground as the boy sprinted toward a line of hedges at the top of a hill bordering the station. With the train thundering behind them, the boy scrambled up the slope, skidding on the loose rocks. Maya reached out an arm and dove forward, fingertips hooking onto the backpack's straps. The boy fell back and lay in the dust, staring up with wide, frightened eyes.

Tearing the bag away, Maya stood panting, not sure what to do next. It was unlike her to do something so rash. She looked back to where the train hid the platform. Her sister was somewhere behind it.

"I'm sorry," whispered the boy, scrambling toward the bushes.

"Yeah, right," growled Maya, anger simmering to the surface. She debated whether to haul him to the police, but as she stared into his frightened eyes, she deflated. *He's just a kid.* With a sigh she turned to head back, just as a rustle sounded deep within the bushes.

The boy stiffened. "Go," he whispered.

"Huh?" muttered Maya.

"Please, go," said the boy, his voice tight. "They're coming. . . ."

Maya backed up, apprehensive at the fear on the boy's face. She was about to turn and run, when three young men emerged from the tangle of bushes and cut off her path. Dressed in jeans and colorful shirts, they struck a menacing pose.

"What do we have here, squirt?" asked the tallest one in a deep, raspy voice, a jagged scar pinching the skin along the right side of his face.

The boy averted his gaze, staring down at his torn slippers.

The chubby one in a yellow tunic, a gold ring glinting in his ear, whacked him on the head. "Answer Babu, you little runt," he ordered in Hindi.

The little boy whimpered, doubling over. "Please, Ladu, sir . . ."

"Hey, stop that!" Maya cried in English, stepping forward.

Babu jerked his head toward her in surprise. "Are you an American?" he asked, frowning.

Maya bit her tongue as the third boy, thin as a wire and with protruding teeth, stared at her. *Don't say anything else,* she told herself, and glanced back toward the station. *Where's Zara?* Before she could move, the one in yellow, Ladu, grabbed the little boy's ear and twisted. "Looks like girlie here isn't going to talk, so I'm going to ask you one more time: Why were you chasing her?"

"She's got money in there," squeaked the boy, tears glistening in his eyes. "Hundreds of dollars—*American* dollars."

The trio stared at Maya, eyes calculating. Babu smiled, twisting his scarred face. "Ladu, Pinto, get her."

11
From the Frying Pan into the Fire

RUN! SCREAMED A VOICE inside her head as the boys lunged for her. Sharp branches scraped her face as she bolted farther up the hill through the bushes, clutching her backpack. Realizing that they'd catch her if she ran back toward the train station, she surprised them by plunging headlong into the hedge. As she pushed through the dense bushes, she felt the ground slope down again. She glimpsed bright-colored lights and heard the din of activity. Heart pounding, she burst through the bushes onto the edge of the city. A bazaar loomed ahead—shops strung with bright neon signs—bustling with shoppers, peddlers, beggars, and families out for a stroll.

Disoriented, she stood a moment, uncertain which way to go. She couldn't go back into the bushes toward the station and her sister—the boys were in there somewhere. She'd have to find an alternative route. *But which way? Left? Right?* The rustle of leaves behind her forced her to make a quick decision. She dashed toward a line of sari shops and then ducked between a jumble of elbows, seeking cover. Glancing back, she spotted the boys emerging from the bushes: Babu, who seemed to be the leader, Ladu in yellow, and the skinny, weasel-faced Pinto. Babu paused on the curb, cupping a cell phone to his ear, apparently having an animated discussion with someone on the other end, while pointing to the boys to split up.

Not wasting a second, Maya slid past a girl haggling over a pair of red sandals and ducked into a side alley packed with traditional leather and silk shoe-vendors. Zigzagging past shopkeepers and customers, she reached an intersection. She stood wild-eyed and sweating, wondering where to go next.

An auto rickshaw sputtered to a stop across the street, unloading a group of young women. As Maya debated what to do, a shrill whistle sounded at the other end of the alley. She glanced back, breath catching in her throat; it was the one in yellow, Ladu, alerting the others. *He's seen me!* she thought. Instinctively, she slipped behind a stack of beaded slippers, trying not to panic, weighing her options. *I can't outrun them. I have to find another way.*

She glanced over at the girls paying the rickshaw driver, and without thinking twice, dashed across the street. "Go," she ordered the driver, jumping inside.

"Eh," said the old man, owl-eyed behind thick, Coke-bottle glasses.

Maya peered back toward the alley and her blood turned to ice. The boys had made it halfway through, shoving aside an elderly man, overturning his stall.

"Just drive," she said in Urdu, huddling in the backseat. "Please!"

With a shrug, the driver revved the engine and bucked forward, the rickshaw emitting a smelly plume of diesel from its tailpipe. Maya twisted around on the slippery vinyl seat and peered through the flaps covering the back window. The boys had skidded to a stop at the curb. They were staring at her, fists clenched, as the rickshaw careened around the corner and disappeared from their view.

Maya slumped forward, gripping her backpack. *It's*

okay . . . it's okay . . . breathe . . . I've lost them, she told herself.

Hunched over his steering bar and muttering to himself, the driver followed a taxi down a wide, open road while behind them rattled a bullock cart, laden with laundry. Her relief soon evaporated as traffic snarled, slowing to a halt. The area ahead had been cordoned off: hundreds of laborers lugged bags of concrete and metal pilings toward a hotel undergoing renovation.

"Where do you want to go?" the driver asked, glancing over his shoulder.

"Train station," she blurted. "Please take me to the train station."

"Which one?" he asked, scratching a wart on his chin.

"Agra Cantt Station."

The driver harrumphed. "You should have told me before," he said. "We're going the wrong way."

"Sorry," Maya said. "Please, just get me there as fast as you can."

"There is a lot of construction," he grumbled. "I'll have to go around it."

"That's okay," she said.

As she sat in the safety of the rickshaw, the reality

of what had happened hit her like a ton of bricks. She slumped, clutching her backpack, tears blurring her vision. *How did that happen? We should have been more careful,* she thought. This wasn't San Francisco, where she and her sister knew their way around. This was India, where things were much more unpredictable . . . and, frankly, dangerous. But as the shock eased, an unexpected feeling of pride buzzed through her veins. She'd outwitted the boys! Wait till she told Zara. . . . Remembering her sister, she realized that she must be out of her mind with worry.

"Do you have a phone?" she asked the driver, desperate to tell her she was on her way back to the train station.

"No," he grunted.

Disappointed, Maya looked down at her watch. There was still time to catch their train. . . . And this time she and Zara would hide in the waiting room, as the conductor had advised. They had a promise to keep.

She leaned forward in her seat, mentally urging the rickshaw to move, but they sat idling at the bottleneck. The poor bull still stood behind them, his long-lashed eyes resigned, swishing his tail, ignoring the honking horns. Maya turned to scour the road behind them, spotting a cycle rickshaw barreling up the asphalt. She squinted . . . and caught a flash of yellow. It was Ladu, legs pumping on the pedals; Babu sat in the back with Pinto, who was grimacing into his phone.

Before she could yell at the driver to go, he found a gap between two trucks and shot forward. Maya's last glimpse of the boys was of them jumping out of the cycle rickshaw behind the bullock cart as Maya's driver maneuvered past the construction site and entered a residential neighborhood, tightly packed with narrow, tin-roofed houses.

As he slowed to let a group of kids get their soccer ball, Maya turned in her seat and peered out the window. *Hurry . . . hurry . . . hurry,* she urged silently, but from around the corner the bull came running, the boys clinging to the back of the cart, its driver and laundry gone.

"Hurry!" shouted Maya, turning to the driver.

"Okay, okay," he muttered, stepping on the gas, increasing the gap between them and the snorting bull. A few blocks ahead loomed a sign, the image of a car with an X marked across the top. The driver slowed and pulled into a large parking lot.

"What are you doing?" asked Maya.

"No autos beyond this point," said the driver. "It is

a government rule to control the bad air. . . . Pollution. So I need to turn around here."

"Okay," panted Maya. "Just hurry."

The rickshaw chugged past a line of parked cars and was about to make a U-turn, when a van pulled out in front. As the driver slammed on the brakes, Maya peered back and her blood ran cold; the bull stood panting at the entrance to the parking lot, cart empty. Frantically, she looked between the cars. There was no sign of them. Then she glimpsed a face reflected in a side mirror of a small hatchback. One of the boys was hiding a few cars down. She wondered where the others were but didn't wait to find out. She bolted from the rickshaw, running at full speed.

"Girl!" shouted the driver. "You need to pay for the ride. . . ."

Pushing aside a feeling of guilt for cheating him, she bent low, weaving through parked cars, desperately trying to shake the boys from her trail. She passed a shuttered tailor's shop and ducked into a narrow lane lined with shuttered shops with signs for pottery, wood furniture, and metalware. Backpack thumping against her spine, Maya turned left onto a wider street, empty of cars—no rickshaw or taxi she could flag to get to the train station.

At the faint whisper of thunder, she looked up; clouds were collecting in the distance, closing over the fat moon perched on the horizon. Within its silvery circumference rose a familiar sight: a tall, thin minaret. *A mosque,* she thought. *Someone can help me there.* She remembered their mosque back home in Berkeley. *Imam* Jackson's gentle face, framed by a grizzled salt-and-pepper beard, flashed in her mind. The religious leader of their mosque, he was a kind-hearted soul who provided counseling in addition to leading prayers and serving as their Sunday school principal. Breathing a sigh of relief, she ran toward the welcoming beacon.

Out of breath, she reached the faded brick structure, a mishmash of columns, arches, and domes, straddling half the city block. Beyond the rusty gates, she found the courtyard empty. Her heart sank. Evening prayers had ended and the place was deserted. Just about to depart, she heard the murmur of voices coming from inside. She ran up the cracked steps, pausing just inside the doorway, where the murmurs grew into shouts. Startled, she hid behind a set of lattice screens that ran the length of the cavernous hall. Assembled at the center of the threadbare carpet sat a group of men.

A bearded young man stood, body rigid. "You

don't understand!" he cried in Urdu, waving a pamphlet. "This new report says that we Muslims are the poorest, most illiterate community in India."

Beside him, a bespectacled, gray-haired man nodded. "Sadly, what Hashim says is not untrue. Over the past fifty years, our community's prospects have fallen—even behind the poor untouchables."

"It's impossible to join the army or get a decent job. I was told in an interview to go to Pakistan, a country for Muslims," said another young man. "Can you believe it? My grandfather fought for India's independence beside Gandhi!"

"That's *exactly* what I'm saying," Hashim said. "We're at the bottom of the heap—left behind as the rest of India prospers and modernizes!"

"Modernity?" barked a plump, white-bearded man in a crisp white cap. "Modernity has brought nothing but immorality, greed, and ungodliness to our beloved India!"

Maybe this isn't the right moment to interrupt, Maya thought as the bespectacled man spoke again.

"Now, *Imam* Farooq, let us not confuse modernity with progress. Progress is achieved through education."

"Indeed," warbled an elderly man. "Even before Partition, Sir Syed Ahmad Khan, founder of Aligarh

University, emphasized the study of science and mathematics."

"Our prophet Muhammad, peace be upon him, urged his followers to seek knowledge, even if it led them to China," shouted a squeaky-voiced boy.

Maya glanced down at her watch, growing more and more anxious. She had an hour to get to the train station—otherwise she'd miss the train. She stumbled forward. "Please," she croaked in Urdu, "I need help."

A wizened old man near the *imam* gasped. "Who dares interrupt our meeting?"

Maya froze, surprised by his angry tone.

"What is she doing out alone this late?" grumbled a voice. "She shouldn't be here—tell her to go home."

As two men beside the *imam* rose, Maya stumbled back. In Pakistan, women didn't usually visit mosques either, not like they did back home in San Francisco, but she hadn't expected such an unwelcoming response.

"You shouldn't be interrupting an important meeting," sputtered the *imam*.

"She's only a little girl," interjected Hashim. "Ask—"

Before he could finish his sentence, Maya stumbled back into the courtyard. If Zara had been there, she would have yelled at them to help, but she just couldn't. *I'll find a rickshaw myself.* . . . Back through the gates, she merged with the dark shadows casting their veil over the deserted street. She skirted a growling dog nosing through a pile of garbage and ran, feeling the wetness of raindrops spattering against her cheeks. Hearing footsteps ring out behind her, she picked up speed, sprinting parallel to a towering wall built from wide blocks of red stone.

Seconds later, she caught the echoes of furious barking as an ominous rumble echoed above. She ran harder, hugging the wall around a corner, where she stumbled upon two uniformed guards carrying heavy machine guns. Startled, she instinctively ducked behind a lamppost. She ignored the rain, eyed the burly guards patrolling past a sign for East Gate, and wondered what to do. Maybe they could help. As she debated whether to approach them, a bright set of headlights turned onto the street and careened toward them.

A sleek silver bus pulled up beside the arched gateway, and through the rain-streaked windows, Maya could make out the ghostly faces inside. The bus door swung open, and a suited Indian man got out and stood at the curb.

"This is not good," he complained loudly, shielding his head with his arms. "We won't be able to see anything with the clouds covering the moon!"

"Yes, sir," said one of the guards as they hurried over. "This is not a good night for sightseeing."

Maya bit her lip, peering past the bus, hoping to see a rickshaw. But there were no rickshaws or taxis, just a line of garbage cans. About to look away, she saw a hint of movement. Then a flash of yellow.

Oh, no . . . She swung around, staring back at the path she'd come from. Standing at the corner, about forty feet away, stood Pinto, breathing hard. Beside him was Babu, slipping his cell phone into his pocket, lips twisted in a victorious smile. They'd been tracking her all along . . . and now they had her cornered.

12

Star-Crossed Love

SCRUNCHED LOW TO KEEP the guards from catching sight of them, the boys slithered along the wall, inching closer to Maya's hiding spot. Frantic, she looked for an escape. Just as she was about to run, lightning flashed, bringing a deluge of rain that obscured her sight.

"This will not work tonight," she heard the suited man shout. "We're going to have to cancel our visit."

The bus, I need to get on that bus, thought Maya, darting from her hiding spot. *They can drop me off at the train station. . . . I need to get back to Zara.* She could see a blurry image of the guards leaning toward the man, who had disappeared from view.

"Wait," Maya called out, but her voice was drowned out by the rumble of the bus's engine. The man had boarded, and the bus was pulling away. From behind her, she could see the hazy figures of the boys running toward her. She approached the towering gate, built into the thick red wall. It was slightly ajar. Filled with indecision, she slowed. Ladu was out there, on the other side of the road. . . .

Without a second thought, she dove toward the gap in the gate.

"You there, boys!" Maya heard a guard bark behind her. "Get away from the gate. No unauthorized entry!"

Maya didn't pause, but sprinted up the stone path. She veered right across an expansive lawn, squinting through the rainy haze, looking for a place to hide. *There.* Across from the immense central courtyard stood a towering two-story building, its roof topped with rounded cupolas at each corner, matching balconies on each level. She scurried through the curved arch, past ghostly white marble designs inlaid in the dark stone.

"Lock the gates. No one is to come through!" came a muffled shout behind her, accompanied by the creaking of metal hinges as the guards sealed shut the gate she'd just passed through.

A set of heavy doors, sheathed with bronze plates, rose ahead of her. *Maybe someone can help me. . . .* Damp and shivering, she pushed on the smooth wood with all of her might. The doors swung inward and Maya ran through, stopping beneath a brass lamp that was suspended from the vaulted roof and cast faint light in a fat circle. Except for the patter of rain, silence greeted her in the sparse octagonal room. Multiple alcoves and doorways stretched out on both sides, and on the right stood a set of glass doors with a sign that read: ARCHAEOLOGICAL SURVEY OF INDIA. Through the glass, she spotted an old-fashioned phone sitting on the table. *I can call Zara,* she thought, eagerly running over. The doors were locked. Hope deflated as she stood shivering in the empty building. The thought of braving the rain and trying to get the guards to open the gates was beyond daunting. She needed time to rest, to think. She knew they'd missed the train— there was no way to get back in time. She wished she could call Zara, let her know she was safe and she was coming back. *I just need the rain to die down,* she thought, feeling completely drained. *After an hour or so, I'll find a way back.*

As she turned, her gaze fell on a wall, sparkling as the light illuminated a dazzling painting of a garden, awash in emerald green, gold, and orange. It was as if she was back with her grandfather, about to prune dark-blue devil's trumpet. She padded forward, and as she got closer she realized that this was not a painting at all. The entire scene was made of semiprecious stones, cut and fit together with brilliant precision, similar to a mosaic. A sheet of glass had been placed on top to protect it from the elements. A set of stairs rose beside it. Hoping to find a hidden spot, she climbed the steep stone steps and reached a narrow passageway on the second level. A small room stood on the left, filled with broken furniture, boxes, and stacks of yellowing papers. On the right was another chamber, larger and with a balcony, its view obscured by a veil of water. The passageway continued deeper into the building, but she had no wish to explore further.

The room on the left was as secure a spot as any to wait out the rain. Legs wobbling, she entered, spotting a switch beside the door. With a snap, the small, square space lit from the flickering bulb hanging from the ceiling. Wet and shivering, she sank onto the dusty floor, panic threatening to overwhelm her exhausted mind. But she couldn't fall apart; she needed to make sense of what had just happened. With shaking hands, she pulled out her journal and a dark grey pencil and took a ragged breath.

Sunday, September 18, continued
Undetermined location

I did something dumb . . . something really, really dumb. I let Zara talk me into going off on our own . . . to find the chest while my grandmother lies sick back at the hospital. Zara said it would be a walk in the park . . . and I fell for it, like I always do. I'm such an idiot! So here I am, stuck God knows where in the middle of Agra because we took the wrong train. What do I do now?

Maya paused to rub her snotty nose with her sleeve. The thought of her sister pacing the platform, freaked out with worry, filled her with fury—but for a brief minute also filled her with satisfaction that Zara was miserable too.

Maya stared down at the words she'd written. They swam around on the page, not making much sense. Trembling, she closed her eyes and lay down on a stretch of old newspapers, clutching the journal. She needed a few minutes to rest and collect her thoughts. She wished desperately that she was back home in San Francisco, under her duvet she'd tie-dyed red and blue. She wished that they'd never had to make that journey to Pakistan . . . that *Nanabba* was not dead.

It was the sound of chattering that pierced Maya's foggy brain. She woke befuddled, and spotted two furry creatures near her feet, glaring at her suspiciously. With a squeak Maya shot up, startling the small, long-tailed monkeys. They shrieked and scampered through the door. Realizing she'd fallen asleep in the musty, cramped room, she remembered in a rush the events of the past twenty-four hours.

After a minute of self-pity, she kicked aside the crumpled papers and got up, squinting down at her watch: 6:07. It had been seven hours! She needed to get back to the train station—for all she knew, Zara had called in the Indian army to search for her. And her mom . . . she must be at the hospital in Delhi by now. She grabbed her backpack and headed to the door. As she was about to step into the passageway, she froze.

Across the hall, framed by the window, stretched the

sky, morphing from indigo to turquoise, streaked with pink and peach as a golden orb rose from the banks of the river. If that wasn't stunning enough, the building that stood glowing in its midst took Maya's breath away. On a raised platform sat tons of gleaming marble the color of snow—a white that meant perfection. It was the Taj Mahal. Her gaze flew up the magical floating palace, up the delicately carved facade to the dome on top. Four towering minarets stood on the corners like protective sentries. She and Zara had seen this building the day before from the train. She darted toward the balcony, floor wet from the rain, and stood openmouthed.

A second later, realization dawned that she could figure out exactly where she was. She fished out her guidebook and opened it to a map of Agra. It pinpointed where she stood, along the banks of the Yamuna River on the east side of the city. The train station was to the west, along Station Road. As she looked for the best route back, she skimmed the paragraphs, stumbling upon the name of the Taj Mahal's builder: Mughal emperor Shah Jahan. This was no palace, she realized. This was a *tomb*.

Overcome with grief after the death of his beloved wife, Mumtaz, the emperor went

*into mourning. He emerged a year later, his
hair white. To commemorate his eternal love,
he commissioned the Taj Mahal. Twenty
thousand skilled artisans, stone carvers,
calligraphers, and gemstone masters worked
for twenty years, creating this masterpiece.
But beneath its breathtaking beauty lies
a secret chamber containing the bodies of
Shah Jahan and Mumtaz.*

Lost in thought, Maya stared out over the mani-
cured gardens, home to a family of monkeys, groom-
ing one another beside the central pool. A monkey
darted into a flower bed, which she saw was filled
with roses—a Mughal favorite—ranging from ivory
to yellow to bloodred, a splash of glorious pink nestled
at the center.

Knuckles white as she gripped the guidebook, she
remembered *Nanabba* talking to her as he pruned:
*Mystics regard the rose as the symbol of divine glory, while
poets profess that it represents the face of the beloved.* Her
grandparents would have loved seeing this, she realized, heart twisting. But the Taj's beauty was tinged
with sadness, for death had taken Mumtaz the way it
had taken *Nanabba*.

Maya squeezed her eyes shut. *Nanabba* had promised to bring *Naniamma* to India and to find the chest, which contained the ring she wanted him to have, even in death. Maya felt the weight of responsibility heavy on her shoulders: She had promised to help fulfill that wish. She needed to get back to the train station, so she and Zara could continue to Faizabad. They *had* to.

A couple came strolling into view and she shrank back. The monument opened at dawn, allowing visitors to view it in the clear morning light. Looking back at the guidebook, she discovered that she'd spent the night in the Darwaza-i rauza, the great gate that led to the Taj Mahal. Pulling on her backpack, she snuck back downstairs and exited through a door leading to an open courtyard. She stood at the steps down to the courtyard, eyeing the three gates that stood to the left, to the right, and straight ahead. She'd come through the East Gate the night before. *Best avoid that one,* she thought. Joining the crowd, she walked toward the busiest gate. She paused near the soldiers' station, but didn't see any of the boys from the night before. She hurried on, knowing she couldn't catch a taxi until she reached the perimeter. She might also find a phone to call her sister, who was probably out of her mind with worry.

As she passed a group of hawkers selling minia-ture replicas of the Taj Mahal, she caught a familiar flash of yellow, and froze. *Ladu!* But it was a bright flag flying from a sweet seller's stall. Spooked, she ran toward the street, but before she could step out, someone jumped from behind a parked donkey cart and grabbed her arm. It was Pinto. Before she could scream, he clamped his hand over her mouth and dragged her toward an approaching bicycle rickshaw. The wiry, bald driver slowed, his skinny brown legs easing up on the pedals. Hard fingers reached down from the rickshaw and hauled her inside as Pinto melted back into the crowd.

1 3

Caught

STUCK BETWEEN BABU AND Ladu, Maya cowered beneath the tattered canopy of the cycle rickshaw, a scream caught in her throat.

"Don't even think of making any noise," hissed Babu, his fingers digging into her shoulder.

"Please," Maya coughed out, wincing as Ladu wrapped coarse twine around her wrists. "Take my money; it's yours. Just let me go."

Babu stared at her and laughed—a harsh, ragged sound. "You don't even know the half of it," he said, and turned away to keep a lookout.

Eyes wide, she stared at the back of his head, fear and

confusion flooding her mind. *What else did they want?* she wondered. Back in Karachi, when her mother had threatened that she would be kidnapped if she wandered away alone in the market, she'd wondered how she would react. She'd thought she'd panic, cry, and fall apart. But now she knew: She'd go numb and her mind would turn icy cold. Crystal clear, as if it were yesterday, she remembered the words of the police officer who'd visited her class the year before.

If you are ever kidnapped, he'd instructed, *try to get away before your abductor can take you to a second location. Watch where you're going and remember the landmarks so you can find your way back.*

So Maya stared out the side of the rickshaw, muscles tense, eyeing landmarks, biding her time as they sped past a herd of goats wandering the early morning streets of Agra. *If he'd just slow for a second, I could jump. . . .* A *chaiwallah* stood across the street. Two women a block down rolled up the shutters at the Bharat Detective Agency: (MARRIAGE FRAUD A SPECIALTY read the sign). Maya desperately tried to meet the women's gaze, but they were too busy. As she searched the street for any sign of help, the driver exited the business district, heading toward a bridge in the distance. *Oh, no . . .* They were crossing over the Yamuna River. Her stomach knotted as she recalled the map. They were going in the opposite direction of the train station!

Catching a whiff of burning rubber, she looked up and spotted smoke rising from beyond the treetops. The driver pedaled on, bypassing a stalled car and turning onto a road crammed with small factories. The air was smokier here . . . and oddly quiet. The driver looked around nervously and Maya knew what he was thinking: *Where's the clang of machinery and the workers?* At the next intersection, they stumbled onto the source of the smoke: the entrance to a sprawling cricket stadium rose in front of them, fires blazing across the pitch inside.

"This is not good," muttered the driver, back-pedaling.

"Hey, hey, what are you doing?" argued Babu.

"I have a bad feeling about this," muttered the driver, making a sharp U-turn. "I'm taking another route." He drove back past the workshops and entered a neighborhood with narrow winding streets, poorly constructed shacks on either side with closed doors and shuttered windows.

As they approached the main thoroughfare, a faint buzz sounded in Maya's ears, which soon grew to a thumping roar. A hunched man ran by, pushing his vegetable cart, not caring as tomatoes splattered on the ground. Right behind him marched a mob—men in bright orange chanting, waving swords and banners.

"Oh, no," said the driver, eyes wide in a pallid face. He lifted the wooden cross hanging around his neck and slipped it inside his faded shirt.

"Oh, bugger," said Ladu.

"Turn around," ordered Babu.

"I'm stuck, boy!" cried the driver, stopping between two parked cars and hopping off. "I'm leaving—you should too. These people aren't to be messed with. They don't take too kindly to those not like themselves when they're riled up. I don't fancy getting beat up, so I'll be back for my rickshaw later."

"Come on," said Ladu, dragging Maya down from the rickshaw while Babu followed with her backpack.

They hid behind a stack of empty crates, musty with the smell of mustard oil. Between the gaps Maya watched two men pass, holding up a sign with the image of a tiger's face along with words in Hindi she couldn't read. A few gathered in the middle of the road, holding a length of green-and-white fabric. As one of them pulled out a box of matches, others unfurled the

rectangular cloth—a green-and-white flag emblazoned
with a star and crescent in the middle . . . the same as
the one on the Pakistan International Airlines flight
she'd flown on. Maya's blood ran cold as the voracious
blaze ate through the material and the crowd danced
in frenzy.

"No Pakistani dogs playing cricket here!" they
chanted.

Cricket . . . Maya remembered her grandmother and
Muhi's conversation. India and Pakistan were about
to play a cricket match in Agra.

"Pakistan not welcome till they turn over terrorists
who bombed Mumbai!" added a barrel-chested man
to additional cheers.

Maya eyed the empty alley beside them, but there
was no way she could make a run for it. "Who are
they?" she whispered, not realizing she was speaking
aloud.

Ladu mumbled under his breath, "Hindu nation-
alists."

Fear pooled in her gut. "The RSS?" she asked,
remembering the member of the group who'd killed
Gandhi.

Ladu gave her an odd look. "No," he muttered.
"They're different, but they believe many of the same

things. All I know is that when they're mad, you don't want to get in their way, no matter *who* you are." He sat back, and while Babu played on his phone, he pulled a tiny picture from his breast pocket. From the corner of her eye, Maya saw that it was a photo of a young woman with a fat baby in her arms. When Ladu caught her peeking, he turned away, his gold earring flashing. So she lay her head on her knees and took a deep, calming breath.

Blinded by a bandanna, Maya winced, jolted by a pothole. She could sense they were getting farther and farther away from the train station . . . and her sister. *Think . . . think. . . . What do I do?*

Once the mob had disappeared, the boys had stolen the rickshaw and pedaled west, through a park within a cluster of renovated colonial buildings, now upscale offices, trendy restaurants, and elegant boutiques. On the outskirts of town, they'd pulled over in a thicket of trees beside an old hotel to tie a bandanna over Maya's eyes. Shrouded in darkness, she could feel the rickshaw circle a roundabout and zip down a bumpy road. Tossed about, she used the chance to push up the fabric, catching sight of sparsely developed land, edged by tall grass and thick hedges. Ladu slowed,

navigating through a gap in the bushes. At the end
of the dirt road stretched a metal fence, topped with
sharp spikes, and beyond a locked, rusty iron gate
stood a derelict two-story building, its rusted tin roof
sloped over a line of smashed windows resembling
broken teeth. Once beyond that gate, she realized
she was at the second location the police officer had
warned her about, and terror bloomed in her heart.

Babu pulled her from the rickshaw, removed the
bandanna, and pushed her toward the tall padlocked
gates. They were unlocked, and before she could even
think to run, she was dragged, knees shaking, across
the dry grass toward the leering structure. Once they
were up the rickety steps, Babu shoved her through
a metal sliding door into a large open space. Maya
blinked rapidly, eyes adjusting to the gloomy darkness. To the left stretched a storage space separated
into different sections. A heap of old clothes was piled
in the back, and beside it was a line of buckets filled
with nuts, bolts, wires, and metal scraps. The largest corner was packed with plastic: plastic bottles,
sheeting, wrapping, and bags. Beside these sprawled a
workshop: tables piled with tools and bulky machines.

As Maya scanned the walls, looking for an exit,
Babu pushed her toward a row of open doors in the

back, but her foot snagged on something soft, tripping her. Babu cursed but kept her from toppling over. When she looked down, her eyes widened. It was a blanket . . . and beneath it a small hand. Dark, tangled hair spilled out onto the floor. Horrified, Maya realized that rows of tiny bodies lay all around.

"Take care of her," ordered Babu, shoving her toward Pinto, who'd appeared like a skulking alley cat. Without a backward glance, Babu pulled out his cell phone and disappeared with her backpack.

Muffling a yawn, Pinto shoved her into one of the empty rooms and locked the door. The room was a small and cramped space, stacked with old, mildewed bolts of cloth. Maya scurried toward an interior window fitted with metal bars, and peered out over the warehouse. She spotted Pinto and Ladu standing near her window, talking in hushed voices.

"Look," said Ladu, a worried look on his round face, "we've got to make sure we do better than last week."

"Yeah," said Pinto nervously, licking his protruding teeth. "Boss looked like he was going to chuck us all out when he learned we didn't make our quota."

"He can replace us faster than we can say 'Bollywood,'" said Ladu. "And man, I've got nowhere to go. I can't go back to my village . . . especially after what they did to my mother."

"Don't worry, man," said Pinto. "We'll be fine."

Ladu gave him a sharp nod, then turned to walk down the line of sleeping bodies, nudging the tiny lumps under the blankets with his foot. "Wake up, lazy butts!" he bellowed. "It's nearly eight o'clock."

"Ow," came muffled yelps, coupled with grumbling.

Fingers curled around the cold iron bars, Maya watched small, weary faces emerge. She stared open-mouthed. *They're kids.* Stories from the newspaper back in Pakistan tumbled through her mind—stories of orphans and runaways, of children sold to gangs by poverty-stricken parents. Heart slamming against her ribs, she saw that one of the boys had a missing arm. Another girl had a leg that lay at an odd angle, like it had broken and never healed properly. She gulped with fear. Gangs in Karachi deliberately mutilated kids so that they would get more sympathy and money when sent out begging. Did these people do the same thing? Panicking at the possibility, she gasped.

"Who are you?" A voice speaking Hindi pierced through her fear. Maya looked down at a little girl in crooked pigtails staring at her with curious, almond-shaped black eyes. Beside her stood an even tinier girl, with a smudged, dirty face and a too-short blue dress. "Who are you?" the larger girl repeated, louder this time.

"Uh, my name is Maya," she responded in Urdu, reflexively adding, "Who are you?"

"I'm Guddi," said the girl, swaying side to side, her small frame enveloped in an oversize pink jean jacket covered with sparkling rhinestones.

"And what about your friend?" Maya asked, eager to talk to someone.

"Oh, this is Mini," said Guddi. "She likes to follow me around."

Mini ducked her head and grabbed a corner of Guddi's jacket.

"Where are your parents?" asked Maya.

"My parents are dead," Guddi said in a matter-of-fact tone. "We lived with my aunt, but she didn't give us any food and beat me when I peed in my bed."

"That's terrible," gasped Maya.

Guddi shrugged. "My brother's clever," she said with an impish grin. "He made a plan for us to run away on a train and we ended up here."

"What are you doing *here*?" asked Maya, trying to figure out who exactly she was dealing with.

"We work here," she said. "We collect stuff . . . old clothes, plastic, metal parts, and stuff."

"That's it?" prodded Maya.

"Uh-huh," said Guddi. "And Boss gives us food and a place to sleep."

"Guddi," hissed a boy with similar eyes, appearing like a ghost. "Don't talk to her; you'll get in trouble."

Maya froze. It was the boy from the train station, the one in the Mickey Mouse T-shirt, the one who'd gotten her into this mess!

"Oh, Jai, don't be such a scaredy cat," sighed Guddi.

"Get moving, you lazy good-for-nothings!" shouted Ladu. "Work begins in half an hour."

Refusing to meet Maya's eyes, Jai disappeared, dragging his little sister and Mini with him. He gently guided the little kids as they scurried into action, picking up blankets and folding them. He and two older girls then hurriedly put together a breakfast of dried bread and steaming tea. Maya shrank back at the edge of the window as Babu strode into view.

"Boss is busy," he told Ladu and Pinto, his raspy voice irritated. "I told him we caught the fat fish like he told us to. But he said he can't come in till later this afternoon."

"That's fine," said Pinto. "The fish isn't going any-where."

"You make sure of that," said Babu. "I'm taking a crew out to the docks."

Babu left with the older kids, including Jai, while Ladu piled the disabled children onto a cart and pushed them out the main gate. As they headed off, Maya realized with a sinking heart that she was the fat fish . . . and she hoped that whoever this *Boss* was, she wasn't going to be gutted for lunch.

14

A Spider's Web

BESIDES THE SINGLE BREAK when Pinto took her to a stinking, windowless bathroom at the other end of the warehouse, Maya had been stuck in her cell all day. She'd tried desperately to come up with a way out; she'd tested the bars on the window (firmly affixed to the ledge), then the door (locked, hinges loose but secure). She peered through the gap at the bottom of the door and felt a loose brick wiggle at the base. There was no other way out. She stood up and spent the hours pacing. And worrying. Worrying about Zara, who was back at the train station worried out of her mind. Had she gone looking for her? Gone to the police? She must have tried to contact their mom by now. If she had, then her mom was probably crazy with worry too. *Oh, man. . . .* It was impossible to get her mind around the whole crazy situation.

Left behind, Guddi and the little ones had washed up after breakfast and swept the floors. Mini followed Guddi around like a shadow, calling out for her when she fell out of sight. Maya had tensed when Babu had returned, his crew laden with bulky gunny sacks. Without a glance in her direction, he'd ordered the kids to organize their haul, creating piles according to type of plastic. While the younger ones sorted, the older kids revved up the machines, shoving plastic in one end and packaging the pellets that came out the other.

At three o'clock Ladu's group arrived, looking sweaty and exhausted. Maya watched their broken bodies collapse on the floor, chests wheezing, lips parched. Guddi came running, practically tripping over her jean jacket, carrying a metal pitcher of water, and Mini passed out glasses and helped them drink. The machines sputtered into silence and they stopped for lunch. Jai and another boy laid a large sheet on the concrete floor as an older girl brought out a large pot and a sack full of bread. The kids crowded into a circle, holding their allotted piece of bread, and a skinny boy ladled *daal*, lentil stew, into metal bowls. Before the steaming yellow mush settled, they dove in.

"What about her?" piped up Guddi, pointing in Maya's direction, which earned a sharp poke from her brother.

Babu looked her way with a sneer. "What, our fat little fish wants to be fed?" He aimed a kick at Guddi's backside. "If you are so concerned, give her yours."

Mini followed Guddi as she came to pass a piece of bread and a cup of lentils to Maya through the bars, along with a bent metal spoon. "Don't mind him," she whispered, rubbing her bottom. "Old Babu just acts like an ornery old cat. It was his drunk old father who cut up his face, you know. Nearly killed him, so he ran away. Now he can't help but be mean."

His own father cut up his face? Maya's stomach twisted in revulsion, pity, and a pang of hunger. She stared at the watery yellow mush, flecked with chilies and pieces of potatoes. Lentils weren't on her miserly eating list, but she didn't totally hate them. "I can't take that," she whispered, staring into Guddi's lean face.

"I'm not going to eat it," said the stubborn little girl.

"But you're hungry," said Maya.

"I want you to have it," said Guddi.

Hunger won over fears of what it might do to her stomach and she scarfed it down.

As shadows lengthened along the ground, Babu paced near the door, looking out into the front yard, checking the time on his phone. Boss still hadn't shown up, and Maya could see the irritation on Babu's face. At the other corner of the hall she spotted Jai, sneakily passing out cookies to the little kids. Cookies she'd given him the day before. She stood, holding onto the bars as another cramp rippled across her abdomen. Within an hour of eating the *daal*, she had begged to be taken to the bathroom, and now, even though nothing was left in her stomach, she still felt like she had to go. . . . She knew she shouldn't have eaten it.

Finally, when the sun hung low on the horizon, a sleek red hatchback came screeching through the gates. The driver hopped out, skinny legs encased in tight jeans, leather jacket hanging loose, black hair slicked back with gel. Eyes hidden behind aviator sunglasses, he sauntered up the stairs and strode inside. "How are my little employees?" he bellowed, bringing the kids to a halt. They looked at him, faces tense. From the corner of her eye, Maya watched

Jai disappear behind a row of boxes, pulling Guddi with him, Mini tagging along. "Bringing in good money?" he asked. Some kids nodded, eyes fixed on the ground. "Good, good. . . . If performance keeps improving, I'll get some nice hot *jalebis* for you!" The man strode on as the kids returned to their tasks with strained smiles. "Babu," he called out, setting the teen scurrying. "How did the beggars do this morning?"

"Very good, Boss," he replied, bowing. "The new girl with the broken leg is a great addition—she was an excellent purchase."

Purchase? Maya's stomach churned as she remembered the sad-eyed girl from the morning, gulping down water, face twisted in pain.

"Cripples are cheap," said Boss with a shrug.

"We should get some more," said Babu.

"I will think on it," Boss said, fingering the thick gold chain around his neck. "The plastic business is getting too competitive. Any loser with a few thousand rupees is opening up a processing outfit."

"But we collected double the amount of plastic from the docks," said Babu. "It will bring in good money."

Boss slipped off his glasses, eyes narrowed. "Are you the boss now?" he asked in a cold, slippery voice. "Making business decisions?"

Babu shrank back. "No, Boss, no . . ."

Boss broke out into a grin. "Good. Remember that I picked you up from the gutter. You can end up back there as quickly as you came."

"Forgive me, Boss," whispered Babu.

"No matter." Boss waved his hand. "I need to focus on our new line of business—the steel magnate's son from Calcutta worked out brilliantly last time; the family ransomed him handsomely." Babu puffed out his chest, looking pleased with himself. "That's why I asked you to pick her up after you called—I'm hoping we get a good amount for her."

"I left you a message that she's here," said Babu.

"Yes, yes, I got it, but I was busy," he said, lips tightening. "Are you *sure* she's not a local? We don't want her family coming down the road looking for us if something goes wrong with the deal."

"I'm one hundred percent sure, Boss," said Babu, vigorously shaking his head. "Like I told you, Jai spotted her at the train station buying a ticket—she was alone."

Maya shrank away from the window, her heart beating wildly. *They're talking about me.* And then it struck. Jai had lied to them. He'd told them she was alone.

. . .

Fifteen minutes later, after another trip to the bathroom, Maya was thrust into a soft leather chair in a room painted the color of lilacs, with framed, autographed movie posters hanging in a straight line on the wall. Boss sat across from her, a shiny desk between them.

"Why does she look so sickly . . . and smell?" he said, wrinkling his nose.

"She got sick after eating some of the kids' lentil stew," snickered Babu. "She's been running to the bathroom all day."

"Tsk, tsk," said Boss. "Get her some of my bottled water I keep in the fridge. We can't have her becoming dehydrated."

"Yes, Boss," said Pinto, running out.

"Welcome, welcome," he said, turning to Maya, revealing straight white teeth.

Maya shivered, tongue-tied, staring in horrified fascination at how the colors of his shiny silk shirt shifted from blue to green.

"Do you like my shirt?" he preened. Not waiting for a response, he added, "It's just like the one Amir Khan wore in his last movie—*Mumbai Nights*. A fantastic film—incredible songs and dance numbers."

"He looked most excellent in that movie," agreed Babu.

As they recalled scenes from the film, Maya surreptitiously surveyed the room; like her cell, this room had a window facing into the warehouse, protected by iron bars. There was no exit to the outside or even a window.

"So, tell me—what's your name?" asked Boss, leaning across the desk, fingers folded.

Maya took a sip of the water Pinto had handed her, staring at Boss like a mouse cornered by a toothy cat. In the blink of an eye, Babu lunged and twisted back her arm, ripping the seams of her shirt. As pain flared through her shoulder, she yelped.

"I don't think that is necessary," tsked Boss. "One can gain more with honey than vinegar. Pinto, how about you go to my car and bring out the box of sweets from the backseat. And get me some tea." Pinto left.

"Now," said Boss, turning back to Maya. "What's your name?"

"Maya," she mumbled, pulling together the edges of her rent shirt.

"Well, Maya." He enunciated the *M* with pursed lips. "How did you come to be at the train station?"

"I was on my way to . . . to Jaipur," she lied.

Boss snapped his fingers and Babu brought over her backpack, dumping its innards onto the desk. Out flew damp clothes, followed by the guidebook and her journal. He unzipped the front pocket and shook again. Slips of paper flew out, along with a flash of dull silver, which fell to the floor. Maya's heart froze, but Boss's eyes were focused on what fell out next: a dark blue rectangle and the hundred-dollar bill. Quickly, she put her foot on the iron key to her grandmother's house, hiding it under her shoe.

His eyes widened as he grabbed the passport. "You're an American?" he asked.

Maya jerked her head in response, panicked. . . . *Where is Zara's passport?* Then she remembered. She'd handed it to her when Zara needed identification to buy the tickets. Momentarily filled with relief, she saw Pinto enter with a big box of sweets.

Conflicting emotions flitted across Boss's face: glee, uncertainty, then a hint of worry. He grabbed a piece of sweetmeat and shoved it in his mouth. Bright orange crumbs fell on his shirt, leaving an oily stain. "Who were you traveling with?" he asked between chews as he separated the wallet and passport while shoving the clothes, guidebook, and journal back into the backpack.

"My sister and my father," she said.

"Where is this sister and father of yours?" he asked, midchew.

"They were at the train station with me," she said with false bravado. She needed to say something to make them let her go. "They're looking for me now."

The man's eyes narrowed. He looked at Babu and motioned him to go. A minute later he returned, Jai in tow. Maya's stomach sank. She'd forgotten that he'd seen her with Zara and no one else.

"You found this girl?" he asked Jai, who stood beside the desk, hands clenched, shivering.

"Yes, Boss," he whispered.

"Tell me exactly what you saw."

"I saw her come off the Jaipur train," he said, tone hushed. "I noticed that she was wearing jeans, but not the cheap kind Babu and Ladu wear. And her tennis shoes—they're the real thing. So I thought she was a foreigner, so I followed her to the ticket booth. She talked like the television show . . . the one with the big houses in California. Then I saw the American money fall from her bag."

"And there was no one with her?" prodded Boss. "Another girl? A man?"

Jai paused, face serious as if he was thinking. "No one, Boss. Just her," he finally replied with a lie, his face blank.

Boss's full lips tightened. Quick as a cobra, he reached across the desk and slapped Maya across the face. The stinging pain bloomed along her cheek, accompanied by ringing in her ears.

"Do not lie to me again," he said, sitting back as Jai's face blanched. Boss offered the box of sweets to him and he took a piece of almond fudge with shaking fingers. "Excellent work, my boy. I see a good future for you here."

Tears slid down Maya's burning cheeks as her stomach cramped again.

The man stared down at her passport and read out her name, age, hair, and eye color. On the next page, under emergency contact information, was her address in California and the phone number. "Now, who will answer if I call this number?"

"My father," said Maya, throat tight.

"Babu, this is quite an interesting situation," said Boss. "A runaway from America . . . one that could net us quite a bounty."

Babu nodded, looking pleased.

"I need to go to the bathroom . . . ," Maya croaked. "I feel sick. . . ."

"Take her to the bathroom and give her more water

and some aspirin tablets. We can't have her getting sick," said Boss, wrinkling his nose. "Then lock her up. I have a lot of thinking to do." He tossed Pinto the backpack.

"Please . . . I need a shirt," said Maya, eyeing the backpack.

"Give it to her," said Boss, dismissing them.

As Maya exited, his voice rang out behind her. "Remember . . . Agra is my kingdom and I am like a spider—its web reaching everywhere. So don't think you will escape."

Cheek throbbing, Maya lay curled up, hugging her backpack and clutching the key she'd snatched as she'd left Boss's office. *Dad's going to have a heart attack when Boss calls him.* Wondering how she'd ended up in this nightmare, she sat up, shaking uncontrollably. *Calm down,* she told herself.

Monday, September 19
Agra, India
The boys found me. They caught me and brought me back to their boss. . . . Now I know why they were after me so bad. . . . They didn't

want the measly hundred-dollar bills. . . . they wanted me . . . a stupid American worth a ton more in ransom . . .

Maya stared at the stark words and oddly thought of Mrs. Hackworth. What would her teacher think if she read this? Would she even get a chance to read this? The reality of what was happening started sinking in and an image of her sister flashed in her mind, accompanied by an acute feeling of loss.

I wish Zara were here—she would know what to do. Even if she didn't, I know she wouldn't go down without a fight. And <u>*Naniamma*</u> *. . . she never lets anything push her down. She survived the train ride to Pakistan . . . survived being an orphan . . . met the man she loved and started a family. And me?*

Maya paused. *What about me?* She'd talked her way into coming to India, navigated through Delhi, escaped the thugs in Agra, and hidden in the Taj Mahal.

I am Maya. Maya the mother of Hermes and Buddha. I am Durga, the invincible one—the power behind the creation, protection, and destruction of the world. I am a pea.

Like an electric current, purpose raced through her as Maya put down the journal to pace the room. She paused at the window, watching the kids finish up for the day, organizing supplies and oiling the machines. Guddi and Jai stood beside the open door, whispering and casting glances toward her room. Anger built up in her chest like a volcano. If it hadn't been for *him*, she wouldn't be here. She glanced away from them, spotting a plume of dust approaching the gates. A jeep pulled in beside Boss's car and out stepped a familiar khaki uniform. A tall man hurried up the steps, cap covering gray hair, pistol strapped to his side. It was a police officer!

15

Bathroom Follies

MAYA WATCHED THE POLICEMAN enter the warehouse through the main doors, swinging his baton. As he passed, the kids shrank aside, disappearing into the shadows.

"Help!" shouted Maya, pressing her face against the bars.

Guddi's head popped up from along the path, but before she could say anything, Jai clamped his hand over her mouth and pulled her behind a sack of trash.

"Please help me," repeated Maya, wondering if he hadn't heard her.

The policeman glanced toward her cell with a frown as he neared.

"I've been kidnapped!" added Maya.

The door of Boss's office burst open and he strode out. "Quiet, girl," he ordered, giving her an irritated look.

"Please . . . ," begged Maya. "I need help. . . . That man is holding me for ransom!"

"Wow, you've got a feisty one this time," said the officer with a chuckle.

Maya's heart sank to her knees as confusion muddled her thoughts. *What?*

"This one is unique," said Boss, rubbing his hands together. "She's an American!"

"An *American?*" said the officer with a low whistle. "I don't know about that. . . . It could bring some serious heat on us. Kidnapping foreigners can prove very troublesome."

Maya stared at the officer, a sick feeling spreading through her stomach. He was one of them!

"I have it under control," said Boss, hands on his hips. "The silly girl was traveling alone—how stupid is that? I'll call her father tomorrow, once I get a few things sorted out. I need your help, like last time, since we'll need a bank account where the money will be wired. With your smarts and connections, it'll be a breeze," he added, buttering him up.

Maya felt like she was going to throw up.

"Once we get the money, we'll drug her like the last kid," continued Boss. "She won't remember much of anything and we'll dump her at the hospital so her family can pick her up."

"We're going to have to change hospitals and bribe another hospital director," grumbled the policeman. "That money-grubbing woman from the last one was complaining that she wanted more for the risk she was taking."

Drugs? thought Maya. *What kind of drugs?*

"Don't worry," Boss soothed. "Now, come into my office—I have your cut from last month's operations. Revenue's up twenty-five percent. I'm sure that will ease your wallet, since your daughter is getting married in a few months. I hear that grooms' families are getting greedier and greedier about dowry these days."

"You're right about that." The officer sighed. "The boy's father has been sniffing around, asking for a car and more cash—can you believe it?"

"What a crook," said Boss.

"And I've got another daughter to marry off," complained the officer.

"Well, the money we get from this girl will cover the entire wedding," said Boss.

"You're right about that," said the police officer.

"Pinto!" yelled Boss, heading toward his office with a chuckle. "Get us some tea!"

"You've really expanded the business after taking over from your father," said the officer, looking around the warehouse as he followed.

"We're moving into the big leagues now," said Boss with a smile.

As the duo entered Boss's office, Maya slithered down the wall and slumped on the floor. She spotted the journal. *Don't give up,* it seemed to say. *Find a way out.* Angrily, she pushed away her empty tin cup, traces of lentils clinging to the rim. Lentils that had gotten her sick. She grimaced, eyeing the bent spoon beside the cup. Then she grabbed it, testing the sharp end. A ray of hope pierced her heart. At the top of her lungs, she yelled to Babu to take her to the bathroom, making sure Boss heard her. He'd make the boys listen to her request. They had to take care of her—she was worth a lot of money to them.

• • •

Maya sat back and glanced at her watch. It was nearly three a.m.—another three hours before dawn exposed her plans. *There!* After hours of digging, it finally came loose: a large, heavy chunk of red brick. *It's now or never,* she thought, staring down at the rows of bodies through the bars. Around ten o'clock, the younger ones had set up their beds and fallen into an exhausted sleep. Babu and the older boys had stayed up, drinking soda and playing cards. Finally they'd wandered into their room on the other side of Boss's office and collapsed on low wooden beds.

"I have to go to the bathroom," she shouted. This was the fifth time that night she had made one of the boys take her, even though she didn't need to go.

A few of the children stirred, but not one answered.

"Hey," she repeated, clanging the bars with the tin cup. "I have to GO!"

"Shut up!" came Babu's sleepy voice.

"I have to go . . . now."

"Go ahead," bellowed Babu.

"I don't think Boss would be happy about that," shouted Maya.

"Pinto," growled Babu. "Take her to the latrine."

"Make Jai, the brilliant mastermind, do it," came his groggy response.

"Jai!" shouted Babu. "The girl needs to use the latrine."

Jai shot up from the floor, a ghostly shape shrouded in a tattered quilt. "Yes, Master Babu," he mumbled, still half-asleep as a metal key flew out the door of the room where the boys were sleeping, and landed at his feet.

"Give her a bucket. She can *tatti* all she wants," came a muffled snort.

Maya's cheeks reddened as Jai stumbled around the shadowy warehouse, finally appearing with a blue plastic bucket. Maya stood on the other side of the door, trembling, holding the brick in her hand. The lock clicked open and the little boy entered, bucket held out in front of him. Maya raised the brick high, aiming for the back of his head.

Jai entered slowly. "I'm really sorry all this happened to you," he whispered in a sorrowful voice.

Maya's hand shook. She felt terrible, but she had no choice. She'd expected Pinto to take her, but it was Jai, and she had to take advantage of the opportunity.

"I just wanted to get your money . . . so I could take care of my sister," he whispered, placing the bucket on the floor. "I didn't know they would kidnap you."

Maya looked down at his tiny body in the shadowy light. *I can't . . . I can't hurt him.*

Jai turned and saw the brick. His eyes widened, then squeezed shut. "Do it," he whispered. "Do it good so they believe you caught me by surprise."

Maya slumped against the wall. "I can't," she muttered, arm falling to her side.

They stared at each other. "I have an idea," he whispered.

A few minutes later, Maya tiptoed from the room toward Boss's office, backpack slung over her shoulder.

"They're definitely asleep," whispered Jai, right behind her. He angled his head toward the boys' room, from where a symphony of snores percolated.

She stopped, catching sight of her passport and the money lying on Boss's desk through the window, guarded by bars. "He always locks it when he leaves," Jai whispered, pushing down on the handle.

A loud creak sounded from the boys' room, and they dove behind a bin of metal parts, waiting for one of the teenagers to come stumbling out. After a few minutes of silence, Jai grabbed her hand and led her toward the row of sleeping kids near the machines. Gently, he woke Guddi. Obediently, she sat up, gingerly disentangling herself from Mini, who'd been clutching her arm. The little girl whimpered, snuggling deeper into the warmth Guddi had vacated. As she put on her precious jean jacket, which she'd been using as a pillow, Jai looked down at the line of little kids, a deep frown tugging his lips. Maya followed his gaze, and for a moment uncertainty flooded her.

What about the other kids? She'd only been thinking of herself. Before she could ponder further, Jai grabbed Guddi's hand and hurried past the hill of plastic toward the metal door. It had been left ajar to let in the cool night breeze, the building secured by locked gates and the surrounding fence. Shrugging aside the niggling guilt in her gut, Maya followed them outside. Cautiously, they descended the rickety steps and ran toward the padlocked gates. Maya climbed up the fence like she did her grandfather's peepal tree, finding footholds along rusty joints, stopping on the top when one of the spikes snagged her shirt.

"Help!" whispered Jai from below, where he stood with Guddi on his shoulders.

Maya straddled the fence and leaned down to grab the little girl's hands. As she pulled, Guddi found her footing and scampered up, Jai following behind. Making sure his little sister made it to the top, he slid down the other side to help her down.

"Come," said Maya, getting ready to go over the top.

Guddi turned, ready to shimmy down, when her jacket caught on a spike, piercing the fabric and barely missing her chin.

"Are you okay?" said Maya, steadying her.

"Oh, no," hissed Jai, staring toward the warehouse. "Hurry!"

Maya squinted toward the building. A tiny figure came tumbling out the doorway.

"Guddi . . . ," wailed Mini. "Don't leave me!"

"Guddi, let's go," croaked Maya.

"I can't," whimpered the little girl. "I'm stuck."

"Take it off," Jai yelled from below.

Maya leaned over and yanked on the thick fabric, but it remained entangled on the spike, tightening further as the little girl squirmed. From the corner of her eye, Maya saw lights flickering through the broken, toothless windows. *The boys—they're awake.*

"We have to go—*now*," whispered Jai hoarsely as Mini reached the gate, sobbing.

Maya desperately tugged the jacket, but it was no use.

"They're coming!" cried Jai, as the metal doors roared open.

16

Friendships Formed

THROUGH THE SCRAGGLY FIELDS they ran, zigzagging around the trees. Veering in the opposite direction of the main road, they stumbled through the shadowy darkness until they came to a small clearing.

Feeling as if her heart would burst from her chest, Maya stopped. She stood panting beside a protective clump of bushes. "Wait. . . . I can't run anymore. . . ."

Jai stood like a robot, stony-faced. "I can't believe we left her . . . ," he whispered.

"We had to," said Maya desperately. "If we stayed, they would have caught all of us. . . . What good would that have done?"

Jai turned to her, fists clenched. "She's my sister! I'm supposed to take care of her."

"We'll find a way to get her, I promise," said Maya, wincing at yet another oath she didn't know she'd be able to keep.

"You don't understand," he said. "I've wanted to leave for months. . . . The stuff Boss makes me do, it's getting worse—I can't do it anymore!" Maya stared at him in surprise as he continued, voice choked. "Every week I have had to bring in a certain amount of money—if I don't, I get in trouble. Two months ago, I stole a thousand rupees from an old woman who'd asked me to help her across the street to the hospital. The money was for her granddaughter's medicine. . . . I found out later that the little girl died."

"But why did you join Boss's gang?" Maya asked, not able to help it.

"When we first arrived in Agra, someone tried to take Guddi from me while we slept on the streets. It was too risky to be on our own. We needed protection and a safe place to stay."

Maya stared at him, reminded again how hard it was for street kids to survive.

"A few days later, Ladu spotted me stealing bread from a corner shop. He told us about Boss's gang and asked if we wanted to come check it out."

"But how did you get to Agra in the first place?" asked Maya.

"My parents left our village last year to find work in the city, leaving Guddi and me with our aunt. In the beginning it was good. They sent money and we were able to go to school, get new clothes, and even have special things to eat, though we missed them like crazy. Then we got a letter. There was a fire at the factory where they worked . . . and they died."

"I'm so sorry . . . ," whispered Maya.

"When the money stopped coming, my aunt stopped caring about us. We were two unwelcome kids no one wanted around. So I took Guddi and I left. . . . And now that I've run away, they're going to hurt her."

"No, no, they won't," said Maya, awkwardly patting him on the shoulder. "They'll be mad at you, not her."

Jai became stony-faced again. "The world doesn't care about you when you are poor and weak," he said. Maya stared at his childish face, his eyes those of an old man who'd seen too much.

"Look," said Maya. "I swear I'll help any way I can. Once we get to the train station, my sister and mother with help you get Guddi, and the other kids."

"It's too far away," said Jai, shaking his head. "We'd need a rickshaw."

Maya nodded, but there was no transportation to be found on the desolate patch of scrub they found themselves in, nor did they have any money. "Let's keep walking, but out of sight from the road."

Hidden by a copse of trees, the duo looked out across the parking lot over to a *dhaba*, a truck stop restaurant. The sun had risen above them an hour before, illuminating a line of trucks parked beside the gas pump. Each was laden with something different: bales of hay, electronic parts, squawking chickens, watermelons, and sugarcane. The rustic restaurant was packed with drivers and motorists, including several families sitting at wooden tables, tucking into breakfast.

"No rickshaws or taxis," murmured Jai.

Maya paused by one of the trees. "Don't worry, we'll find one. But first I need to talk to my sister."

"There must be a phone down there," said Jai, a calculating look in his eyes.

Maya nodded, praying for the strength to do what she needed to do. She stared up at the leafy branches and was surprised to see that it was a peepal, a sacred fig tree, like the one she'd enjoyed climbing in her grandfather's garden. Her grandfather had explained to her that according to legend, the Buddha had attained *bodhi*, or enlightenment, while meditating underneath such a tree. Desperately seeking enlightenment herself, she glanced at Jai, who was staring quizzically at her tennis shoes, which were caked in dirt. Kneeling down, he brushed away some dead leaves near her feet, revealing a black square of leather.

With a wide grin, he flipped the wallet open and a thick wad of rupees spilled out into his palm. *Thank you, God!* Maya's heart raced at this stroke of good fortune. As they stood trembling behind the tree, footsteps approached, accompanied by guttural mumbling. Maya pulled Jai back and peered around the trunk, where a tall, burly man in a sky-blue *shalwar kameez* paced, surveying the ground, hand clutching his green turban.

"Aye, Guru," he muttered, praying. "God is One. All victory is of the Wondrous Guru." Maya and Jai shrank in the shadows as the man kicked stones with his sandaled feet. "Where is it?"

As Jai clutched the wallet, a debate raged in Maya's head. *Keep it; you can take a taxi directly to Faizabad,* said a voice, while another challenged, *You can't steal!* After hesitating for more than a minute, she grabbed the wallet from Jai, whose eyebrows shot up. She crept from behind the tree, wallet outstretched.

At first the man stared at her hand, then looked at her face, eyes puzzled. "Aye, how did you get this?" he asked in Punjabi, which Maya somewhat understood since the language was a cousin of Urdu and Hindi.

"It was on the ground. . . . I found it," she said, as Jai popped out behind her.

He looked at them, a thoughtful frown pulling his heavy eyebrows together. "Thank you," he muttered, sticking it in the pocket of his *kameez*. "My wife would have my head if I arrived back home without my pay." Then he turned to leave. Before Maya could retreat into the trees, he whipped back around. "Have you two eaten?"

Maya shook her head.

"My name's Bhagat. Bhagat Singh. Come," he said, and trudged toward the *dhaba*.

Maya stood for a moment, frozen. *Don't talk to strangers,* echoed her grandmother's voice. But Jai was off, weaving through the tables where the families sat busily eating. It was better to think what to do on a full stomach, she reasoned. They sat across from each other at a picnic table as a waiter arrived, bearing a tray piled high with steaming *puri* (fried bread), potato curry, omelets studded with green chilies, sweet *halwa*, and tea, all piping hot. Without a word they dove in.

"Are you a truck driver?" Maya asked a moment later, trying to make polite conversation while Jai sat blissfully stuffing his face with sticky, sweet *halwa*. Only a *puri* and some potatoes for her, and a sweet cup of tea.

Bhagat nodded as he sopped up potatoes with *puri*. "Been driving for over ten years—I know the roads of India like the back of my hand."

"Are we close to Faizabad?" she asked eagerly, trying to gauge how far they had to go.

"Faizabad is east of here, about seven hours away," he said. "I've been there many times. It's a nice city, but it's had its share of trouble the past few years."

"Are you going there?" asked Maya hopefully.

"No, I'm headed to Patna," he said. "I'm delivering a load of sugarcane to the mill."

Patna, thought Maya with growing restlessness. She remembered seeing it on the map in the guidebook. It was the capital of the neighboring state of Bihar, probably another few hours east of Faizabad.

"Where are your parents, your family?" Bhagat asked, eyes narrowed as he washed the tips of his fingers from a tin cup of water.

Maya tensed. "Oh . . . they're, uh, coming."

"Coming from where?" he probed.

Before he could get more suspicious, she stood up. "Thanks so much for breakfast, but we have to go."

"Wait," said Bhagat with a frown.

But she and Jai were already scurrying away, back toward the trees. When they were safely hidden behind the tree trunks, Jai tucked a *puri* filled with egg into his pocket. But it was what was in his other hand that made Maya's breath catch in her throat. "Where did you get that?"

"From her," he grinned, still chewing, pointing back toward the woman at the table across from Bhagat.

It was a cell phone.

"Oh my God!" Zara screamed in her ear, making Maya wince. Then the questions began. "What happened to you? Where are you? How—"

"I got kidnapped," interrupted Maya.

"What? Are you—"

"I'm fine now, safe," added Maya. "And I have our

backpack, so all I need is a ride back to the train station."

"Maya," said Zara, her voice falling multiple octaves. "I'm not at the train station."

"Where are you?" asked Maya.

"A lot happened since you disappeared," she said. "I'm at the police station."

"What?" Maya said, fear settling over her. "Why are you at a police station?"

At the word "police," Jai's eyes widened and he shook his head. "Don't trust the police," he hissed.

"When I couldn't find you, I needed help," explained Zara. "The stationmaster called the police. They looked all over for you, but you'd disappeared."

"Don't trust the police," said Maya.

"What? Why?" said Zara.

"The police, some of them are in on the kidnapping scheme," said Maya.

"What? Are you sure?" asked Zara, her voice falling lower.

"Yes, I'm sure," said Maya. "Just meet me at the train station. We need to get going if we're going to find *Naniamma's* chest."

"Wait, about that . . . ," said Zara, her voice cracking. "After you disappeared, I kind of freaked out. I called Mom—she'd reached the hospital in Delhi.

When she found out you were missing, she hired a car. She'll be here soon."

"Mom's here?" said Maya, giving Jai a thumbs-up. "That's great; she can come with us."

After a second of silence, Zara said, "I don't think that's going to happen."

"What do you mean? Why not?" asked Maya.

"Mom is furious," said Zara. "She's mad on top of mad: us sneaking off to India, *Naniamma* getting sick, us taking off, and then you disappearing. . . . There's no way she'd go looking for the chest."

"What?" cried Maya. "But we're so *close.*"

"I know, I *know*," cried Zara. "But I was *wrong*," she continued, surprising Maya. "It was a stupid, dangerous idea to go running off by ourselves—look what happened to you."

"But I'm okay," said Maya. "And Faizabad is only seven hours away. . . ."

"Look, I nearly lost you," said Zara. "You're my little sister—I couldn't live with myself if something happened to you."

Maya's eyes widened; she'd never heard her sister talk this way. "Nothing that bad happened to me," she said, trying to make her sister feel better. "We're meant to do this—to find *Naniamma's* treasure."

"I know," sighed Zara, "but we're in enough trouble as it is. We can't take off again."

Maya squeezed her eyes tight and took a deep breath. All her thoughts came into sharp focus. She knew what she had to do. "No," she said forcefully.

"Huh?" Zara said. "What's gotten into you?"

"We promised *Naniamma* we were going to get her chest. And that's what I'm going to do," she said adamantly.

"Mom's going to be here any minute," said Zara, "and she's not going to let us go anywhere."

Mom is going to be there. . . . Good, thought Maya, a plan materializing in her mind. "Zara," she said, voice resolute. "I'm going to Faizabad, to the hotel *Naniamma* booked—Maurya—"

"But—," Zara tried to interrupt.

"I'm going!" yelled Maya, shocking her sister into silence. "I will be at the hotel," she repeated. "Mom won't have any choice but to follow me there. Once we're in Faizabad, it will make no sense *not* to go to *Naniamma's* old house to look for the chest."

After a moment of silence, Zara whispered in a small voice, "Okay."

17

Honorable Intentions

THE HUM OF CARS from a nearby road broke through Maya's dreamless sleep. *We've stopped,* she thought, disoriented. She peered past the cardboard boxes into the driver's cabin. Empty. She shook Jai awake while slipping on her backpack. After her conversation with Zara, Maya had texted her the Maurya Hotel's address, then turned to Jai and offered him a deal. If he helped her find her grandmother's chest, she would do everything in her power to get Guddi and all the other little kids at the warehouse. Reluctant at first, Jai realized that with Maya and her family at his side, they would be far more successful. So he'd agreed. After a handshake, they'd watched Bhagat amble off to the bathroom after a third cup of tea. Quickly, they'd snuck over to the parked trucks, inspecting their contents: tomatoes, electronics, hay . . . sugarcane. They'd crawled into the back of the truck, fashioning a hiding spot under a stack of cardboard.

From the map, they knew he'd be driving right past Faizabad. All they had to do was get him to stop so that they could get off. Minutes later, the engine had rumbled to life and they were on their way, passing fields covered in marigolds, kids fishing in a wide pond. . . . Lulled by the sway of the truck, Maya dozed off, clutching the journal to her chest, the pink phone in her hand in case her sister called.

Now, Maya scurried toward the back of the truck. "Something's wrong," she whispered as Jai followed, rubbing his eyes. Together they peered around the canvas flap, catching sight of a low-slung concrete building. A red-and-blue sign on top blazoned: POLICE STATION—LUCKNOW CENTRAL DISTRICT. "Oh, no," said Maya.

"We need to get out of here," whispered Jai as Bhagat emerged through the front door, a slim, silver-haired police officer at his side.

Maya glanced toward the main road, congested with

traffic. If they ran that way, they'd be seen within seconds. She glanced down at the truck's muddy tires and thought fast. Jai's hand clasped in hers, they jumped, and slithered under the truck.

"Good idea," whispered Jai, wincing as pebbles dug into his knees.

"They're runaways, you're sure?" came the officer's voice a moment later.

Mouth dry, Maya recalled the police officer at the warehouse. *Don't trust him.*

Bhagat's sandals and hairy toes came into view, beside gleaming black boots. "Yes, I'm sure," grumbled Bhagat. "Do you think I was born yesterday? She's a foreigner—American or maybe British, I couldn't tell which. She kept using English words and her Hindi was pretty bad. There's a boy with her and he doesn't look related."

"Maybe she's lost?" queried the officer, contemplating the situation.

"No. A lost kid would be upset, wanting to find her parents," replied Bhagat. "For some strange reason she's set on getting to Faizabad, and I got worried about her."

"It's good you brought them here," said the officer.

"Well, I couldn't let her go running around the

country on her own; it can be dangerous," said Bhagat. "They snuck into the back of my truck and I let them think I didn't know they were there."

"Well, let's get her out and ask her what she's up to," said the officer, walking toward the back of the truck.

Maya's heart caught in her throat. She watched the truck driver's sandals disappear as he climbed aboard. She was furious that Bhagat had brought them here, but at the same time she couldn't help but be touched by the fact that he was worried about what happened to them. For a brief second, she wondered if he'd help them get to Aminpur if she told him what she was really up to. But staring at the crisp crease in the police officer's trousers, she knew it was too late for that. If the police were involved, even if he was a good cop, he wasn't going to let her go on some wild goose chase. He'd make her call her mother to come get her. And Maya had come way too far to give up now.

As the truck shook, Jai grabbed Maya's arm and pointed. Nodding, she followed as he slithered forward on his belly.

"Where are they?" asked the officer, growing suspicious.

"I don't know," muttered Bhagat. "They were right here, asleep, when I left."

Emerging from beneath the front of the truck, Maya saw that a river flowed behind the police station. No escape that way unless they swam for it. Parked beside the truck stretched a row of police jeeps, parallel to the main road. Maya and Jai shared an anxious look. *It's now or never,* Maya thought. With both men busy searching, Maya and Jai darted through the parking lot, using the jeeps as cover.

They paused beside the last vehicle in the lot, a bullet-riddled van, and caught a glimpse of Bhagat sticking his head out the back of the truck. "They're gone!" he bellowed in irritation.

Jai grabbed Maya's hand and pulled her forward, running along the shoulder of the road, where a line of trucks rattled along beside them, stacked with lumber. A tiered building loomed ahead—reminding Maya of a wedding cake—topped with an umbrella-shaped dome. As Jai passed beneath a sign on the padlocked gate that encircled the building, she glanced back and saw Bhagat and the policeman standing at the edge of the parking lot, scanning the road.

"We have to hide!" she cried.

Jai nodded, realizing they were exposed on the naked stretch of road.

"There." She pointed toward a line of buses standing at a bus station.

"No," said Jai. "We don't have any money to buy a ticket, and if we sneak on board, the bus driver will toss us out."

They ran past the depot toward a lush stretch of green—a park of some sort? They ran across the road, dodged a motorcycle, and leapt onto a stone path toward the park entrance. Once through the arched gates, they paused to catch their breath. Maya peered around the stone wall toward the police station.

"They're coming," she gasped, spotting a green turban bobbing in the distance, and a flash of khaki.

"This way," said Jai, dragging her up the stone path.

Shaded on both sides by old trees, the path took them deeper into the park. Around the bend they slowed, surprised to see empty, skeletal brick buildings rising on either side, with gaping holes where windows and doors had been. A blue-and-white sign declared the structure on the right to be Dr. Fayrer's House.

"What is this place?" muttered Maya, skirting an old cannon sitting at the entrance to a squat, cream-colored building. She squinted, reading the sign hanging outside: BRITISH RESIDENCY MUSEUM—CLOSED. At the center of the clearing languished another set of ruins, a sprawling ochre building ravaged by cannon and musket fire. Most of the walls had collapsed and Maya could see its innards, the remnants of a once grand villa. Side rooms branched off wide central halls, fitted with spacious balconies and lofty pillars. A feeling of unease settled over her as she glanced back up the path they'd come; it was empty. "They're not behind us," she said.

"We need to get back to a main road," Jai urged.

"Wait a second," she said, stopping in the shadow of a tamarind tree, thick with pods of sour fruit, and extracting the guidebook from her backpack. "Look," she said, pointing down at a map of Lucknow.

> *Lucknow saw the last days of Muslim rule in India when the British deposed Wajid Ali Shah, the last nawab of Awadh, in 1856. This fueled the 1857 mutiny, and the city is best remembered for the ordeal of its British residents during a five-month siege of the British Residency.*

As she peered at the legend for "British Residency," the date rang a bell in her mind. *Naniamma*'s words came rushing back: *In retaliation, Indians rose up in mutiny all over India, in the 1857 war of independence.* "We're here," she said, pointing to the northeast corner of the city.

"There's a main intersection there," Jai noted, then gave her a questioning look. "From there we can figure out how to continue to Faizabad."

"Yes," said Maya, jaw tense. "Faizabad is a few hours from here and we *will* find a way to get there. My mom and sister will be waiting for us."

Book tucked away, they ran toward a dense thicket of trees to the west. Once through the tightly growing trunks, Jai paused, stumbling upon a jagged piece of marble sticking up from the ground. Maya's gaze fell on the inscription:

John Snowdon—Here lies the son of Empire who tried to do his duty. A few feet farther sat another pillar of granite: *Simon Merriwether—Do not weep, my children, for I am not dead, but sleeping here.*

"What is this place?" she muttered, startled. She stared across the field and saw hundreds of similar stones.

"Look," whispered Jai, pointing at a ruined church, its steeple tilting to the right. It stood like a solemn guardian, keeping an eye over the vast graveyard they had stumbled upon.

"Let's get out of here," urged Maya.

She'd nearly made it onto an overgrown path on the other side of the cemetery when she heard a curse come from near the church. Her eyes met Jai's and they both dove for cover. Huddled behind a large headstone, she formed a tight ball in its shadow. Footsteps approached, and she prayed they would keep going. But it wasn't so. On the other side of the headstone, they stopped.

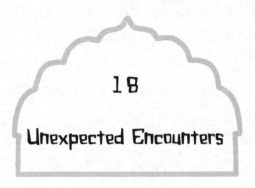

18

Unexpected Encounters

"My dear, are you lost?" quavered a voice, its accent distinctly English, though the words were in Hindi.

Maya's heart pounded. She curled up tighter, hoping that the eerie voice would go away, thinking she was losing her mind.

The voice above cleared its throat. "It's all right, child, I won't hurt you."

She cracked open an eyelid and found watery blue eyes staring down at her, sunk into a wrinkled, sharp-featured face between large ears.

"Uh, yes," she blurted in English, thinking fast as

she sat up. "I was visiting with my family and somehow we got separated."

"Oh my goodness," said the man, switching to English. His linen suit hung from his thin frame. "How could they have just *forgotten* you?"

"Well, I was with my sisters . . . and cousins. . . . There're so many kids that we're always losing someone."

The man paused, a frown adding to the score of wrinkles. "Are you a Yank?" he asked, eyeing her quizzically.

"A Yank?"

"From the United States of America."

"Um, yes," said Maya, eyeing the path, hoping to catch sight of Jai. The longer she dawdled, the more the likelihood of being found by Bhagat grew.

"Those Americans made some fine automobiles," said the man, a faraway look in his eyes. "I still remember my father's Tin Lizzie. . . . Have you ever seen one?"

Maya shook her head.

"A Tin Lizzie is a Model T Ford—my father had one imported from Canada. She was a thing of beauty— shiny Brewster green, stunning curves. . . . But I ramble on," he said, his gaze sharpening. "I am Sir

Arthur Cecil Labant, at your service," he said with a short bow. "That's my wife." He pointed to the grave where Maya sat.

Horrified, she rolled away, catching a glimpse of the inscription on the headstone. *Amelia Labant: 1924–1946. If tears could build a stairway and memories a lane, I'd walk right up to heaven and bring you home again.* "I'm so sorry," she sputtered, smelling mothballs as she stood beside him.

"She doesn't mind, do you, dear?" he said, laying a bouquet of pink roses on the headstone.

"Rosa bourboniana," remembered Maya.

"Why, yes," said Sir Arthur with a pleased smile. "These were her favorite."

"I helped my grandfather plant them in his garden," she said. "They were his favorites too."

"A man with good taste," he said, a twinkle in his eye. "Is he here with you?"

"No, he died recently. . . ."

"So sorry for your loss," he said with a sigh. "When my Amelia died, I went into deep mourning—didn't come out of my room for months. We'd been married a scant year but had known each other since our salad days. Our fathers, bless their souls, were managers with the railway, connecting Bombay to Calcutta."

"Oh," murmured Maya, trying to edge away, but he didn't take the hint.

"When I emerged from my room, India was a country divided . . . no longer the beloved land of my childhood."

"Partitioned?" Maya blurted, then mentally kicked herself. She was supposed to end this conversation, not extend it.

Sir Arthur's eyes took on the glazed look again as he stared at the British Residency, jutting up from above the trees. "James Scott Labant, my illustrious forebear, arrived in India as the writer for records of state with the East India Company. It was 1798, a decade from the day the British had been booted from American shores." Maya inched away while clearing her throat, trying to get Jai's attention. He was nowhere to be seen. But Sir Arthur pinned her with his gaze and she froze. "While your first president, George Washington, battled over the future of the new United States, the British East India Company dug its heels into India. Its army defeated the Mughal emperor and the *nawabs* of Lucknow and Bengal."

Maya blinked and mumbled, "Oh," while he continued talking.

"It was a heady time for James, as we've read in his

letters to his wife. He fell in love with the country, you see," rambled Sir Arthur. "But things took a terrible turn on June 4, 1857. Sepoys attacked their British officers all across India and mutiny blazed."

You mean the war for independence? Maya thought, feathers ruffled as she channeled *Naniamma's* indignation at what the British had done.

"Here in Lucknow, the siege of the British Residency lasted months. Over two thousand English sheltered here, including women and children, many perishing."

Maya's stomach knotted as she eyed the line of graves. They marked casualties of battle that began the unrest that would lead to Partition a hundred years later. From the corner of her eye, she glimpsed a dark head behind a cherub statue. *There,* she thought with relief, inching toward it. Jai's head popped up and their eyes connected. He pointed toward the path and she nodded.

"The British recaptured Lucknow, buried their dead, and kept the Union Jack flying night and day for the remaining ninety years."

"Well, it's been lovely," said Maya brightly, "but I need to go find my family."

"Would you like me to drop you off at your hotel?" asked Sir Arthur, changing the topic.

Maya thought fast. "I don't quite remember which one it is. . . . Palace something or other."

"You don't remember?" asked Sir Arthur.

"I, er, hit my head," she said, pointing to the cut on her head. "My memory is a bit blurry."

"What about a telephone number?"

She shrugged, watching Jai inch toward the path.

"Oh dear, this is quite a predicament," said Sir Arthur. "I'm afraid I don't have those newfangled cellular telephones everyone is carrying about these days. But you're welcome to have a spot of tea with me, rest a bit, and hopefully your memory will jog itself. If not, we can call Inspector Muneer, a good friend of mine from the police station."

Maya gulped at the mention of the police. The last thing she wanted was to talk to a police officer. She eyed the frail, trembling man, recalling *Naniamma's* advice not to ask strangers for help. But they needed to get out of here, and fast. A car ride out of the British Residency sounded like a good idea. She looked toward Jai and motioned him to come over. "That would be very kind of you," she finally said.

19

A Spot of Tea

WITH THE AID OF a cane, Sir Arthur led Maya and
Jai down a dirt path and to the street, toward a sleek
silver coupe parked under a baobab tree. When Maya
had introduced Jai as a family servant, Sir Arthur
hadn't blinked an eye. And when the old man had
asked Jai in Hindi where Maya's aunt lived, Jai had
given him the blank, addled look of a halfwit. Thinking fast, Maya had told Sir Arthur that Jai was a mute
and didn't speak. So with a shrug he'd agreed to take
them both.

"Here she is," he said proudly. "She's a Yank too,"
chuckled Sir Arthur. "A 1957 Studebaker Golden

Hawk. Used to race it with my friends, and no one, not even Dr. Manfred's Bentley or Nawab Patallia's Jaguar, could keep up with it."

The driver's-side door swung open and out slid a hunched, white-haired man in a faded black suit. "Sir Arthur, you've finished early."

"Well, Frank, I've run into a young lady who's in a spot of trouble," said Sir Arthur. "I found her in the cemetery, quite lost. And she can't remember which hotel her family is staying in."

With drooping, hound dog eyes set in a dark-featured face with aquamarine eyes, Frank took in Maya's tangled hair and dirty clothes, a frown settling between his brows. "I see," he murmured.

Maya had a sinking feeling Frank didn't quite believe her story, but it didn't matter; this was her ticket out of the Residency and away from Bhagat. Frank pulled open the passenger door and Maya and Jai slid inside, scooting along the springy leather seat toward the gearshift. Sir Arthur folded his frail body beside them and Frank revved the engine, reversed, and merged onto the road. Maya hunkered low, peering past Sir Arthur's hawkish profile toward the river, watching the multitiered building they'd passed barely an hour before.

"Magnificent, isn't it?" asked Sir Arthur.

Maya nodded, spotting the board she'd just run past. Written in bold letters was: CENTRAL DRUG RESEARCH INSTITUTE. Beneath was a plaque with smaller type: ARCHAEOLOGICAL DEPARTMENT OF INDIA—CHATRI PALACE RENOVATION PROJECT.

Maya slid lower as they passed the bus station, catching the glint of the sun's rays across the water as it sank into the horizon. It would be dark within the hour. A hot breath expelled itself from her lungs as they passed the police station—no sign of Bhagat or the officer. A line of squat concrete apartment complexes floated by, and Frank took a right down a shadowy street lined with a row of genteel, aging Victorian bungalows, languishing behind overgrown hedges. Soon the car pulled up to a set of tall iron gates. In response to the bellowing horn, a wiry old man in shorts appeared to open them. The car purred up the path, past a rambling garden to a dilapidated two-story villa lined with dusty windows.

"Come, my dear," said Sir Arthur, exiting the car.

Maya and Jai followed him up the steps to the porch, its sloping roof held up by engraved columns. She shared a worried look with Jai as the man in shorts efficiently locked the gates.

"Miss Smith, we have company," Sir Arthur called out as they stepped into the expansive foyer. A dusty chandelier hung above, illuminating the rose-patterned wallpaper, cracked and peeling. A wooden staircase curved up to the second floor, lined with a series of portraits of stern-faced men in fitted jackets and silk cravats.

A tiny old woman in old-fashioned black skirts popped in from a side door. "Sir Arthur, you're back early."

"Yes, yes. I have a young lady joining me for tea. If you would be so kind as to tell the cook to have it served in the library."

She stared at Maya quizzically, her blue eyes strikingly similar to Frank's. *They're brother and sister,* thought Maya. Anglo-Indian, a mix of English and Indian blood.

"The cook died five years ago and his son ran off with the silver," Miss Smith reminded him, smoothing back strands of white hair that had escaped her bun.

"Oh, right," said Sir Arthur.

"But I will get it," she chirped, disappearing in a whirl of crinkling satin.

Jai's eyes widened as they stepped into the library,

which occupied half of the first floor of the house. Since passing through the front door, he'd hung back, following them like a ghost. He trailed behind as Sir Arthur led them over moth-eaten tiger pelts, past bookshelves crammed with leather spines, and below the mounted heads of big-horned sambar and smaller, spotted chital deer.

Against the window sat a heavy teak desk, designed with dozens of cubbies, filled with stationery and fountain pens. Leaning against a dictionary teetered an envelope. Maya squinted at it, catching a glimpse of multicolored paper, but before she could examine it further, Sir Arthur guided her toward a dusty grand piano, groaning under the weight of hundreds of framed photographs: shots of tennis matches, tea on the cricket field, and elephant hunts. One in particular caught her attention. A young couple in their wedding finery, smiling ear to ear, eyes sparkling. *Sir Arthur and Amelia.*

"This one was taken in London," said Sir Arthur, pointing to a miserable-looking young man with floppy ears, standing in front of Big Ben. "My father sent me to Cambridge to study law. I hated every minute of it—the awful headmaster, terrible food, querulous students, and the blasted, endless rain."

Maya glanced behind the piano and saw a dreamy-eyed young man looking down at them, resplendent in a medal-encrusted uniform, crown, scepter, and sword.

"With old George at the helm, the Empire crumbled," muttered Sir Arthur, catching her gaze.

"Who was he?" asked Maya as Jai surveyed the room, discreetly making his way toward the windows, looking for a way out, she hoped.

"King of England and the last emperor of the colonies," grumbled Sir Arthur, pacing. "He never should have been king to begin with, but his older brother Edward abdicated for that divorced American, Wallis something or other. What a scandal that was." Pensive, Sir Arthur moved toward the windows. "Everything had all been going so well till then—well, the second great war put pressure on things, but we had done so much for India."

Maya stared at him, uneasy at his growing agitation. "We made agricultural reforms, built industries, and connected the country with rails, roads, and canals," said Sir Arthur, staring at her with haunted eyes. "We brought law and order and rid the country of suttee—widow burning—female infanticide and child marriage. . . . I don't understand how things went so wrong . . . why the people turned against us. . . ."

He was interrupted when Miss Smith entered, carrying a heavy tray. Placing it on a table with a thump, she poured milk and steaming tea into delicate china cups marked with spidery cracks. A plate of limp cucumber sandwiches and cookies sat beside it. "Enjoy it before it gets cold," she urged, and retreated from the library.

"Come, you must be famished," said Sir Arthur, helping himself to a cookie. He settled into the sofa, while Maya took a rickety arm chair facing him.

Maya eyed the sandwich and took a cookie instead. It looked like it came out of a box from the store. She passed another two to Jai, who was sitting on the floor as if invisible. The steaming sugary tea slipped down her throat and pooled warmly in her belly. Nania-mma *was right. It does make you feel better,* she thought, taking another calming sip.

Eyes clear again, Sir Arthur sheepishly brushed crumbs from his lap. "I must apologize. I've been a terrible host, burdening you with such things."

"Nommmph," Maya said through another slurp, which Sir Arthur took as an invitation to keep talking.

"Now, the weather, on the other hand, has been a breath of fresh air. . . ."

Maya half listened to him discuss the importance

of monsoon rains while she scanned the room, trying to figure out the best way to sneak away. The
shadows outside were growing longer and it would be
dark soon. With a sense of panic building in her chest,
she glanced back at Sir Arthur, who'd gone strangely
silent. He'd fallen asleep.

Jai tugged on her arm with urgency. "We need to
leave now," he whispered.

Maya nodded, about to rise, when Miss Smith
appeared. She spotted Sir Arthur's slumped form and
sighed. "Oh, the poor dear, he's nodded off. Won't
be up till the morning," she added, turning toward
Maya. "Come, I'll set up a room for you upstairs."

"Actually, I think we should be going," stammered
Maya.

"Considering Sir Arthur is asleep and Frank has
locked the car for the night, I don't think that would
be advisable," said Miss Smith.

"It's okay," said Maya. "Really, we don't want to be
a bother. We can find our way back to the, er, hotel."

Miss Smith gave her a worried look. "I'm afraid the
streets aren't safe for children on their own. Sir Arthur
would never forgive himself if something happened
to you, or me for letting you leave."

Maya stared at Jai with dread, but he gave her a

wink that seemed to say, *Go with the flow.* Gritting her teeth, she nodded with a forced smile.

The housekeeper guided them upstairs to one of the many rooms along the hall, old keys jutting from ancient locks. Pushing open the third door from the left, she ushered them into a musty room that looked like it had just recently been dusted, but not with much care. "The boy can sleep down in the kitchen," she said, and bustled Jai toward the door. "Have a good night's rest. We'll find your people in the morning."

Maya nodded, gingerly sitting on the edge of the bed. Jai would be back as soon as the housekeeper was asleep, she knew. With her journal and pencil in hand, she began to pace, the thoughts in her head falling into place in purple strokes, which she hoped would bring her a creative solution to the current pickle she was in.

Tuesday, September 20
Lucknow, India

Somehow I got away from Boss . . . and it was because of the boy who tried to steal my backpack. Jai. He helped me escape . . . but we had to do something terrible. We had to leave his little sister behind. I think he is the bravest person I've ever met. He's had a rough life, dealt with things I can't even imagine, but he is so brave that being with him makes me feel that I can do brave things too.

I know it sounds crazy, especially after what I've been through—maybe it's because of what I went through—but I feel I totally HAVE to find Naniamma's chest. We promised her, and Nanabba can't be buried without his ring—he just CAN'T.

Also, I did something I couldn't have imagined I could do. I found the right words to tell Zara that we were going to find that chest, and that she and Mom were coming . . . and unbelievably, she said yes. With Jai's help I've continued on my journey, but I'm stuck again, in a city called Lucknow, eighty miles from Faizabad. . . . Now I just need to figure out how to get there.

A few hours later, the door opened with a soft click. Jai stood in the doorway, a grin on his face. In his hand he had a stack of multicolored bills—more than a thousand rupees.

20

Fighting Pink

THE MAIN BUS DEPOT was abuzz in the predawn hours as Maya and Jai sat in an air-conditioned bus. Luckily, they'd gotten tickets for the first bus to Faizabad and as soon as she'd boarded, Maya had asked the driver if he knew where Maurya Hotel was located. With a smile of recognition lighting his warm features, he'd promised to drop them there, as it was down the road from the bus depot. They'd found seats directly behind the driver's seat. Maya pulled out the pink phone and called Zara, twice, but got voice mail both times. The battery was running low, so she turned it off, praying that her mother and sister were on their way, or were already there.

She still couldn't quite believe they'd made it out of Sir Arthur's house without waking anyone. But before slipping out the front door, as Jai had begged her to do, she'd snuck back into the library, tiptoeing past Sir Arthur lying curled up on the sofa, where someone, probably Miss Smith, had taken off his boots and covered him with an afghan. Squashing the pang of guilt for taking his money, she stopped at the desk where Jai had taken the money. She ripped Sir Arthur's address from an envelope in a pile of mail, vowing to return the borrowed money as soon as she could. Finally, with a last glance at the old Englishman, they'd left.

The journey was coming to an end and she could feel *Naniamma's* chest within her grasp. But she wouldn't have been able to make it this far without Jai. She glanced over at him, heart swelling with gratitude. His face pressed against the glass, he sat exhausted, staring out the window.

"Are you okay?" she asked, knowing that he was thinking of his sister.

"Yeah," he muttered, running his finger along the foggy glass.

"It'll be okay," said Maya, although she wasn't quite so sure herself. "My mom and sister will be at the hotel, and once we find the chest at my grandmother's house, we'll head back to Agra . . . to Guddi."

"Okay," said Jai, apprehension still deep within his eyes. He pulled up his feet and curled up to sleep.

As the bus pulled away from the station, Maya glimpsed the police station and was filled with a deep misgiving about how things had ended with Bhagat. The truck driver had just been trying to help. Was he worried about them? She sighed. There was no way to tell him they were okay. She pulled *Nania-mma*'s memory map from her pocket and smoothed out the wrinkles. The precise handwriting instructed her to arrange for a car at Maurya Hotel that would take them to Aminpur Township. It sounded simple enough, but so far, nothing on this trip had been simple. With a sigh, she closed her eyes.

"Girl." The driver's voice broke through Maya's sleep, jerking her awake. "We'll be at the hotel soon."

"Thank you." Maya smiled groggily.

Gently shaking Jai awake, Maya stood and pulled on her backpack. As she moved toward the door, a wiry dark hand grabbed her arm. The hand belonged to a white-bearded old man in a loincloth and saffron *kurta*. As she looked at him in bewilderment, he angled his head out the window, toward the river running beside them. "That's the sacred Saket, you know," he said, rheumy eyes intense. "This is where Lord Rama left the earth for the divine abode."

"Oh . . . ," mumbled Maya, not knowing what to say as she stared at the sign of the trident on his forehead—three lines of ash, marking him a *sadhu*, or a holy man who'd renounced worldly possessions to spend his life in prayer.

"I'm here to join the liberated souls that dwell here," he said with a gap-toothed grin. "Even old Buddha came here, seeking enlightenment."

He was about to say more when the driver interrupted. "Miss, your hotel is coming up."

"Daughter," said the *sadhu*, releasing his grip. "May you find what you seek, for I see a great longing in your soul." And just as quick, he was back to staring out the window and counting his wooden prayer beads.

With a nod of thanks to the driver, Maya and Jai disembarked. Beside them rose Maurya Hotel, a cream stone building lined with glittering windows. It sat nestled on a street bordered by office buildings just coming to life. The pace in Faizabad was markedly quieter, less frenetic than Delhi or even Agra.

"We made it," grinned Maya, flooded with relief.

Jai nodded a little less enthusiastically, rubbing the sleep from his eyes.

"Come on," said Maya. "Let's see if my mother is here. We can have a nice hot shower and a *big* breakfast."

At the word "breakfast" Jai perked up, and they headed through the main entrance. For a second Maya stumbled, catching a glimpse of her reflection in the glass doors. She was a mess: dust-smudged face, matted hair, dirty jeans, and a ripped shirt. Although she knew she looked like a street urchin, she made a beeline through the empty lobby to the front desk. With as much confidence as she could muster, she asked if a Mrs. Agha had checked in.

"No, I'm afraid not," said the clerk, examining the computer screen.

Maya's shoulders sagged. She hadn't realized how desperately she'd been hoping to find her mother there—to be able to put down the burden she'd been carrying—and to find *Naniamma*'s chest and help Jai get Guddi back. Hiding her disappointment, she combed through the backpack, looking for the hotel reservation slip, but it was missing. "Wait, did a Ms. Tauheed check in?" she blurted out, thinking her mother might have used her grandmother's name.

Thin-lipped, the clerk examined her from head to toe, a frown settling between his brows. "I see that there is a reservation under that name," he said. "But you were supposed to arrive two days ago, on September eighteenth."

"Uh, well," Maya mumbled, thinking fast, "we were detained in Delhi due to, er, food poisoning. Can we still have the room?"

"Yes, but I will need a little time to have one prepared," he said.

As he typed on the computer, Maya pulled out the cell phone and turned it on to listen to the voice mails. Guilt filled her as she realized they were all for the poor woman they'd stolen the phone from. She dialed her sister's number, but after several rings it rolled over into voice mail. Frustrated, she left a message telling her they'd arrived at the hotel. She turned to Jai, who was watching two men having a heated discussion in the corner. Something niggled in the back of her mind. *This is too easy,* she thought. *Why didn't the desk clerk wonder why I was alone? Or ask for my passport like they did at the Taj Palace Hotel in Delhi?* She tried to relax, telling herself she was being paranoid.

Hanging up the phone, the clerk handed Maya two

coupons. "Please enjoy a complimentary breakfast at the hotel restaurant while your room is readied."

Taking them gratefully, Maya and Jai washed up in a restroom off the lobby and headed to the restaurant across from the front desk, where a waiter seated them at a table nestled behind decorative trees strung with lights. A minute later they sat drinking steaming teas. As Maya took a soothing sip, she froze, then blinked. *It can't be.* She coughed, hot liquid burning her throat.

"Oh, no," gasped Jai, eyes wide.

From across the lobby strode Babu. He tossed the clerk a fat envelope, which the man quickly pocketed, and headed toward the restaurant. Jai slid from his chair, dragging Maya with him.

As if watching a jigsaw puzzle coming together before her eyes, Maya realized what had happened. *Stupid, stupid,* she berated herself. The hotel reservation slip had fallen from her backpack in Boss's office, and they must have found it. On it were details of where they were headed—Maurya Hotel, Faizabad. Boss had sent the boys to find her. Perhaps they'd bribed the desk clerk to inform them of her arrival, then lain in wait.

"We can't use the front door," hissed Jai.

"That way," whispered Maya, glancing at the swinging doors to the kitchen used by the waiter.

They shot out from under the table and ran. Footsteps sounded behind them. A quick glimpse revealed Babu slipping into the restaurant.

The duo barreled through the swinging doors, startling two men chopping ginger and garlic.

"Exit—where's the exit?" she panted.

A cook paused in midstir, steam billowing up from the giant pots on the stove. He pointed his spoon past the fridge down the hall.

Without a thought to thank him, they careened past crates of onions and tomatoes and down the dark corridor toward the white rectangular door. With a quick push, Maya burst out into bright sunlight. As she paused, trying to orient herself, a hand clamped down on her shoulder. She turned and saw it was Ladu, and beside him stood weasely-faced Pinto, who grabbed Jai in a vicelike grip.

"Look what our net has caught," said Babu, bursting from the back door a few seconds later. "A couple of fat little fish."

Before she could scream, Ladu's calloused palm clamped across her lips. Fear coiled through her stomach as Babu flipped open his cell phone and dialed.

"Boss," said Babu, "it was just like you said—she

was at the hotel." After a moment, he concluded, "Okay, we should be back by late tonight."

Maya twisted in Ladu's grasp, trying to wrest away, but his grip was too tight.

"Not this time, fish," said Babu, giving her cheek a sharp pinch. "That's for making me look like a fool."

"The car's coming around the back," said Ladu, pushing Maya up the narrow alley, skirting piles of garbage.

Maya recoiled, heart racing as Pinto dragged along Jai.

As they neared the main road, Babu slowed. He angled his head, listening. Then Maya heard something that sounded like a roaring wave, like the Pacific Ocean back home. *Weird,* she thought as a cycle rickshaw passed in front of them. Before she could make eye contact with the driver, he picked up speed, as if trying to get away from the noise. Babu slipped out of the alley, waving at the boys to proceed with caution. As Ladu shoved Maya forward, she paused, openmouthed. It was as if a frothy pink sea had been painted using a wide brush. Like an impressionist painting coming into focus, the colors shifted, revealing coral saris, fuchsia *shalwar kameezes*, and rose-colored veils. And for a second, the warm colors filled her with hope. It was a group of women, all dressed in shades of pink.

"It's that blasted Gulabi Gang," Babu growled, eyeing the women nervously.

Maya frowned. *Gulabi* meant "pink," and *gulab*, "rose." Whoever they were, they called themselves the Pink Rose Gang. *Rosa bourboniana*, her grandfather's favorite. The memory sent a flicker of sadness through her, but also a flash of anger—anger at being caught by the beastly boys again.

"We can't mess with them," muttered Ladu.

"Where's the car I ordered?" growled Babu, peering down the road.

Whoever they are, the boys are scared of them, Maya thought, as Pinto propelled them toward a shuttered stall and stood guard. Maya peered past Pinto, straining to see what was going on.

The leader of the gang knocked on the front door of a house across the street. "Open up!" she yelled, her long braid swinging. "We know you burned up your daughter-in-law because her family wouldn't pay you more dowry."

Maya's blood ran cold; she'd heard of stories like this, of brides burned because they didn't have enough dowry—money or goods the bride's family gave to the groom at the time of their marriage. She reached out and grabbed Jai's hand, staring at the inspiring waves of pink.

From somewhere deep inside her, a courage wound its way through her heart. "This is our chance," she whispered into Jai's ear. "Just follow me, okay?"

Jai's eyes widened, but he nodded.

With a deep breath, Maya pulled back her foot and let it fly, catching Pinto at the back of his knee. As the boy toppled over with a cry of pain and surprise, Maya slipped past and ran into the sheltering sea of pink, dragging Jai behind her.

21

The Last Leg

COOL WIND WHIPPED AGAINST her face as Maya swerved past a pothole, pedaling as if rabid dogs were snapping at her heels. His arms wrapped around her middle, Jai clung to her back, periodically looking behind him to see if they were being followed. But there was no one. The moment Maya had realized that the boys were scared of the Gulabi Gang, a plan had formed in her mind. She knew that if they could make it into the women's midst, they'd be safe. Weaving through the chanting women, they'd exited on the other side of the road. Maya had spotted a rusty black bike leaning against a drugstore stoop. Without thinking twice, she'd jumped on, hoisting Jai up behind her.

They'd traveled in silence until they'd ended up along the main road hugging the river.

"Stop," said Jai, voice subdued. "I need to pee."

While he found a shrub to take care of business, Maya sat on an outcropping of rock, letting the hum of the currents soothe her nerves. She pulled out the cell phone and dialed Zara, but still no one picked up. Worry pooled in her gut. They couldn't go back to the hotel; it was too dangerous. She texted a message asking her to meet them at *Naniamma*'s house, leaving out the details of what had happened with the boys. She didn't want to worry them more than they already were. She also texted Zara pictures of the memory map that instructed how to get to the house.

With a worried sigh, she stared across a peaceful aquamarine stretch of the river. A Hindu temple stood on a sandy beach, its pavilion providing shade to a row of meditating *sadhus*. Bodies covered in ash, two wiry figures carried a statue down to the river. It was Lord Rama. Its deep blue skin triggered a memory—of walking with her grandmother and sister in Delhi, stumbling upon the temple that had led them to Sunehri Mosque. Although it had been a few days ago, it felt like a lifetime. So much had happened since then—so much that she hadn't anticipated—but somehow she had found the power within herself to come this far. Maya remembered the man's words from the bus. *May you find what you seek. I see a great longing in your soul.*

"It's twice I've gotten away from them now," a subdued voice said beside her.

Maya started, turning to Jai. He had a drawn, worried look on his face. The exhilaration of escaping Babu had gone. "I know you're worried about Guddi—," she said.

"I shouldn't have come," he interrupted, eyes bright with unshed tears. "They'll do something terrible to her. . . . They might sell her!"

"No, no, they won't," said Maya, grabbing his hand. "Look. Even if you'd stayed, you knew you needed to get away from them. But where would you have gone? Back on the streets?" Jai's lips tightened at the truth. "You'd be back in the same spot as you were when Ladu found you. You'd have no protection and something more terrible could happen to you or Guddi."

"We're not like you," Jai shot back, eyes flashing. "We are not important—foreign and rich. People don't care about us—whether we live or die."

Maya froze, his words a slap across her face. *He's right,* she thought, ashamed. Her life flashed before her eyes, her privileged life: her house, her loving parents—everything about it was so different from Jai's, or the lives of children on the streets of Karachi. "I care about you . . . what happens to you," she said, her voice tight.

"Why should you? I'm nobody," said Jai, face set.

"You're brave and smart," Maya said. "Without you I couldn't have even imagined doing the things I did."

"I wasn't smart enough to save Guddi," said Jai, adamant.

"No matter how smart you are, going back on the streets on your own is not the answer," said Maya. "So I swear to you, as soon as my mom gets here, we're going to find Guddi."

Jai stood, a flicker of true hope flitting across his face.

"Will you keep helping me?" she asked.

Finally, he nodded.

Maya smiled and pulled him in for a hug, which he resisted, but only for a moment. They stood in silence, comforted by the burble of the water beside them, which reminded Maya of another meaning of her name: eternal spring.

A few minutes later, she pulled out *Naniamma*'s map and spread it out on the rock. "Look, the notes say that the road to Aminpur branches off from the clock tower at the center of town, near Faizabad Jail."

"We'll need to go back into town," said Jai.

With a renewed sense of urgency, they climbed on the bicycle and pushed off.

Through bites of a sandwich, a helpful taxi driver pointed them in the right direction. Clinging to the edge of a busy road, Maya zigzagged through a herd of cows, one of which had decided to sit down in the middle of the intersection.

"Gulab Bari . . . Gulab Bari," Jai kept muttering in her ear, eyes roving ahead as he sat behind her on the bicycle.

The taxi driver had told them to take a right at the famous Gulab Bari, "Garden of Roses," which housed the tomb of an illustrious *nawab* who'd made Faizabad a hub for commerce and trade. From the corner of her eye, Maya spotted the sign for Faizabad Jail. She slowed. According to *Naniamma*'s notes, this was where her great-grandfather's friend Ashfaqulla Khan, along with other freedom fighters, Ramaprasad Bismil and Roshan Singh, had been hanged after an attack against the British in 1927.

"There," Jai suddenly shouted into Maya's ear, making her wince. He pointed toward elegant gates set in a tall pockmarked wall.

Through the bars, Maya could see a lush rose garden and a cream-and-gold mausoleum rising from its midst. Maya nodded and stuck out her right arm to signal her turn. True to *Naniamma*'s memory, the clock tower stood straight ahead, waiting for them. The hands on its face were about to strike four as she wove through people crowding the vegetable market, carrying baskets of leafy greens, cucumbers, eggplants, and squash.

Past the market she took the third road to the left of the clock tower. It led them to the edge of town, where the clamor and confusion ebbed, and they merged onto Nawab Yusuf Road, which ran parallel to the river. A blue-and-white sign with arrows pointed to various destinations: Lucknow, Ayodhya, Nawabganj, and *Aminpur*. Another 4.5 kilometers. They were getting close!

The shimmering waters of Lake Talwar reflected the sun as it hung low in the sky. According to *Naniamma*'s notes, Aminpur sat on the northeast side of the lake. But as the road curved around a bend, the first line of squat concrete shops appeared. Jai's arms tightened around her middle as she pushed on toward the main bazaar, her legs aching from the strenuous ride.

"There," cried Jai, spotting ghostly minarets rising in the distance.

"Great," said Maya, wiping sweat from her forehead. She'd told him to look for a mosque, and there it was. Ignoring her protesting legs she pedaled past a small bazaar, keeping an eye out for the old primary school her grandmother had attended as a child. As the minarets came closer, she saw it—a freshly painted board hanging outside the gates of a tidy school, its front yard empty. Two teachers exited, carrying satchels full of books.

She breathed a sigh of relief. *We're going the right way.*

A quarter of a mile down stood the mosque, abandoned and in disrepair. Goose bumps rose along Maya's arms as she remembered the little picture of a building with minarets her grandmother had drawn on the memory map: This was where the road led to the heart of the old Muslim part of town. According to *Naniamma*'s notes, her old house was situated on a prime parcel of land sitting beside the lake, where she went swimming as a little girl with her sisters and cousins. Maya pedaled up the road as it wound back toward the lake, and rode up alongside a scraggly park. Old villas sat placidly in a row, like old matrons sunning themselves, their backs to the lake, facing the dusty grass.

"It's one of these," whispered Maya, sticking out her legs to stop.

As Jai slid off, she parked the bike in the shade of a tree, across from a posse of boys playing cricket. Laughter filled the humid air as the ball escaped and rolled over to Jai, who picked it up and tossed it back. Jumping up to catch it, a wiry kid gave them a friendly grin and returned to his friends. Maya pulled out the dog-eared note as Jai looked over her elbow.

"It looks like it's this one," he said, pointing to an *X* over the drawing of a boxy house.

Maya nodded, looking from the drawing to the fifth house from the mouth of the street. She stood with her hand in her pocket, clutching the key, not quite believing she was there.

"So what are we waiting for?" asked Jai, kicking a stone in impatience.

She ignored him, savoring the moment as the sun sank lower.

"It's going to get dark soon," complained Jai, crossing his arms over his chest.

Maya squared her shoulders, then stepped onto the road, Jai at her heels. Together they counted the houses until they stood in front of a two-story villa, ivy clinging to its walls. Shuttered windows lined the second floor like a row of aging, ivory teeth, but Maya only had eyes for a large metal lock embedded in the weathered wooden door. She walked up the path to the door, but as she reached out to insert the heavy iron key, she detected the distinct smell of smoke and cooking. She frowned. This was no empty, neglected house. Like her great-uncle's house back in Delhi, it appeared to have new owners. She couldn't just unlock the door and walk in—it would be rude, and maybe even dangerous.

As she stood on the stoop, debating what to do, a flash of white appeared at the window above. Blinking, she stared up, but before she could see who it was, heavy curtains fell back in place.

"Who was that?" she asked Jai, but he shrugged.

She took a deep breath and rapped on the door. After another round of banging, a gaunt man opened it a crack and stared at her with a glaring red-rimmed eye.

"*Namaste,*" said Maya in a rush. "I'm Alia Tauheed's granddaughter. She used to live here, in this house. Before Partition."

The eye narrowed, suspicion clouding the dark pupil.

"She left something here," Maya said in a rush. "Something I need to collect."

"Not possible," growled the man. "No one by that name ever lived here."

"B-but . . . ," Maya stuttered.

"Go away," shouted the man, "before I call the police." He slammed the door.

Maya stood shaking. *Police . . . no police.*

"He's a liar," spat Jai.

"But he said no one by that name lived here," said Maya, throat tight with tears.

"Let me see that map of yours," said Jai. He guided her back to the tree and examined the drawings as she sat slumped against the trunk. "This is definitely the right house," he said, pointing down at the diagram of the street *Naniamma* had drawn. The back of the house had waves, indicating the lake. The back garden had an *X* where the tree they were looking for stood. "This is definitely it."

Maya nodded, anger replacing fear. "Then we have to get into that house."

Jai nodded. "Yeah, we'll figure out how to do it. I didn't live with the best-known thieves in Agra for nothing."

22

Digging Up the Past

MAYA AND JAI HUDDLED near the back gate of her grandmother's villa, listening to the household finish their evening chores and turn in for the night. After the old man had slammed the door in their faces, Maya had stood, petrified, until Jai had grabbed her arm and dragged her away. Since the straightforward approach hadn't worked, they needed a plan B. "Once everyone in the house falls asleep," he'd whispered, "we need to sneak in and dig up the chest." Realizing that they didn't have another choice than to become thieves, Maya had reluctantly agreed.

Now she sat with her back against the wall, staring

at the moon, hanging full and plump, the same celes-
tial satellite that had overseen her mad dash across
what seemed like half of India. Now they were so
close. She glanced over at Jai, who was biting his lip
and leaning against the wall. He was thinking about
his little sister, she knew. She wanted to reach out
to comfort him, but there was nothing to say that
she hadn't said already. She just had to live up to her
promise that they were going to get Guddi. And for
that, she needed her mother, who should have been
there hours ago. *Where are they?* she pondered for the
thousandth time. *Did something bad happen to them? Did
they run into Babu and the boys?* From one worry her
mind raced to another. *How is* Naniamma *doing back
at the hospital?* All the uncertainty was making her feel
like she was going to throw up.

Slowly the flicker of the last gas lamp extinguished,
leaving the cracks between the door dark and silent.
Jai poked her in the ribs, his crooked white teeth
flashing in the darkness. "It's now or never," he whispered, helping her stand up.

Beside them, next to the wooden gate, was a stack
of odds and ends they'd collected from the river's
edge; bricks, boxes, and chunks of wood, assembled
to make enough of a step to help them climb over the

gate. Maya gingerly climbed up first, then hooked her hands over the edge and hauled herself up. Straddling the wall, she leaned down and grabbed Jai's small hands and pulled him up. For a minute, they sat gazing down into the leafy garden spread out beneath them. Along the wall grew a mixture of ornamental flowers and shrubs; to the left, squash vines grew up a trellis, providing shade to a vegetable patch. But it was the trees Maya was interested in; nearly half a dozen rose from various spots throughout the garden. Beyond the treetops she glimpsed a tiled veranda hugging the side of the house. For a moment, the silence comforted her, and she imagined *Naniamma* there as a little girl, running across the veranda into the house, playing with her sisters.

She should be seeing this, Maya thought, her breath catching in her throat.

Jai poked her with a sharp finger, breaking through her disconsolate thoughts. He angled his head to the right, pointing to a soft patch of grass.

Maya nodded, and then leapt, tumbling toward shadowy bushes. She froze beside the profusion of small ivory flowers, inhaling the familiar scent.

Pointy elbows and knees landed beside her. She

paused a moment to let Jai nuzzle the tiny petals. "Jasmine," he whispered. "My father would bring my mother a wreath to wear in her hair." Shaking his head as if to clear it, he scrambled forward, probing the windows, looking for any sign of life. "What kind of tree is it?" he asked.

"Guava," said Maya, recalling the notes. Her great-grandmother had planted it with *Naniamma* just a year before Partition. "It has a deep gash at its base. Oh, and the letters *RMT*—my great-grandfather's initials—are carved into its lowest branch."

"Okay," said Jai, and they hurried toward the first tree, five feet away.

It was a mango, young and supple, not what they were looking for. Their tree would now be more than sixty years old, thick and hard with years of growth. The next tree was also a mango, older and filled with ripe fruit. Beside it branched a leafy sandalwood. They zigzagged through a line of drying clothes toward a gnarled tree hunched over a chicken coop, its branches weighed down by small greenish orbs. Hope burst in Maya's heart and she scurried forward, sniffing the familiar astringent scent of *Naniamma's* favorite fruit. Reaching the trunk, they investigated

its rough bark. Maya's hungry eyes scoured its length. *The gash!* She pointed it out to Jai.

Agile as a monkey, Jai climbed, inspecting the branches as he went. As the tree had grown, the bottommost branches had reached the middle or even the top of the tree. But after several minutes, his face appeared, hanging upside down, marred with a deep frown. "I don't see any initials," he whispered. "I looked all over."

Maya stood, biting her lip. "Well, it's pretty dark up there."

"The branch could have broken off." Jai shrugged.

Maya nodded. "According to the notes, we have to dig."

With a small shovel and trowel they found in a shed behind the chicken coop, the duo got on their hands and knees and burrowed into the thick soil as quietly as they could. Sweat pooled at the base of Maya's spine as the mound of dirt beside them grew. But after over an hour and a half, they'd excavated a hole four feet deep and found nothing but gnarled tree roots, rocks, an empty glass bottle, and an old slipper.

"Are you sure this is it?" asked Jai, wiping his forehead, leaving a streak of mud.

"That's what my grandmother's notes say," said Maya.

"Was it buried directly under the gash?" prodded Jai.

Maya shrugged, stomach in knots. "It wasn't so specific."

"She probably thought she'd be here and would remember it herself," he stated astutely.

Maya nodded. *She should be here.*

"Let's dig on the other side," Jai suggested helpfully.

After another two hours of digging, they'd gone three feet and hit a chunk of concrete. They moved clockwise to another spot and dug. Nothing.

"Are you sure it's this tree?" asked Jai, exhaustion lining his face.

Maya nodded, her throat tightening. *Was* Naniamma *wrong? Did she dream up the whole thing?* The horrible thought settled over her chest like a boulder. She'd come all this way, risked so much, and had nothing to show for it. Nanabba *will be buried without his ring!* She crumpled beside a mound of dirt, mind in a daze, not noticing the shovel drop from her fingers. *I've failed* Naniamma. *And* Nanabba . . . , she thought, her mind numb. There was no chest. No engagement ring, pictures, mementos, or memories. It had all been a huge mistake. Tears blurred her vision and a great sob built up in her throat. Somewhere in the house, something stirred and faint sounds of movement filtered out into the stillness of the early morning. Dawn was fast approaching and they'd completely lost track of time.

"Maya," whispered Jai, tugging on her hand. "We have to *go*."

His voice barely registered in Maya's mind. When light flickered in the veranda window, a sense of danger penetrated her sorrow and she scrambled up, wiping her nose with a muddy sleeve. Jai crouched protectively beside her, holding the trowel like a weapon as the veranda door swung open with a bang. Footsteps echoed across the tiled floor as Maya and Jai huddled behind the guava tree. A man crossed in front of them, heading toward the chicken coop with a basket. Maya tensed; it was the same man who'd opened the door the day before.

"Come on!" Jai grabbed her arm.

They jumped up and turned to run back toward the gate, but in her rush Maya's foot caught in one of the holes they'd dug. She stumbled, taking Jai down with her just as the sun peeked over the lake.

23

Unexpected Encounters

"They're nothing but thieves, I tell you," growled the old man. Maya cringed, holding tight to Jai's hand as they stood shoulder to shoulder on the veranda, surrounded by what looked like every family member and servant in the house. They'd all come tumbling out into the garden in their nightclothes, rubbing their eyes as shouting erupted outside.

"And they dug up all these holes around the tree?" asked a rotund woman, unbound hair flowing over her shoulders.

"Yes," said the old man. "I caught them trying to

run away. When I saw the girl's face, I remembered her from yesterday."

"Are you sure it's the same girl?" asked a mustached man with heavy cheeks, pacing in a white undershirt and crumpled shorts.

"Yes, yes," grumbled the old man. "I'm old, not blind."

"You don't understand," said Maya, her tongue finally unhinging itself from the roof of her mouth. "We're not thieves—"

"You were up to something," interrupted the mustached man.

"You have it all wrong!" cried Maya, panic building in her chest. She remembered the key and pulled it out. "This house once belonged to my grandmother. Here is the key—"

"Ha," laughed the heavyset woman, hands on her hips, glancing toward the mustached man. "This is my husband's house and always has been." A barefoot little girl stood behind her, peering at them through the folds of the woman's hastily wrapped sari. With a last wide-eyed look, she scampered back into the house.

As the woman raged on, the line of sleepy-eyed children huddled near the door moved to the side and out emerged a tiny figure in a snowy-white sari.

She resembled a bright white dove, her delicate features framed by closely cropped silver hair. "Hush," she said, voice resonating with authority.

The stout woman stopped in midsentence, mouth hanging open, which she shut with a frown.

The mustached man stepped in. "Mother, don't worry yourself with this nonsense. Go back to your room; we can take care of it."

"Don't *mother* me, young man," scolded the woman, in a surprisingly deep voice for such a diminutive body.

"You will only weaken your heart . . . ," mumbled the man, cheeks reddening.

"My heart is just fine," said the woman, sailing forward. She stopped in front of Maya and Jai and reached out to cup Maya's chin with a hand marked by spidery veins. Lips pursed, she narrowed her eyes and turned Maya's face with strong fingers, as if examining a peach for blemishes.

Maya blinked, staring into dark eyes that radiated intelligence, and a hint of mischievousness.

"Show me the key," ordered the woman, a deep crease above her brow.

With shaking fingers, Maya handed it over.

The woman examined it from one end to another. "Come with me," she said abruptly, taking Maya's elbow.

"Where are we going?" squeaked Maya, grabbing Jai's hand.

Without answering, the woman pulled them through the line of children back into the house. They stopped at the front door, then slipped back outside. As Maya and Jai watched, the elderly woman inserted Maya's key into the hole and turned. The metal head caught on the latch and spun with a loud click. She glanced back at Maya in surprise. A riot of emotions played out across her face: excitement, sadness, and joy. She opened the door and guided them back inside, ushering them upstairs to a heavy wooden door at the end of the hall. Once inside, she slammed it shut and locked it. She stood panting, as if she'd run a marathon, back against the door, eyes closed.

For a moment, fear flared through Maya. *What have I gotten myself into now?*

"What are you going to do to us?" said Jai bravely.

But the woman smiled. Maya frowned, but her muscles relaxed. Something about the woman's odd manner and the twinkling warmth in her eyes reminded her of *Naniamma*. She calmed down, but just a bit.

"You just wait and see," said the woman, and stepped toward a heavily carved armoire standing beside the window.

As she pulled open the door and rummaged through the shelves, Maya glanced out the window. Early morning light filtered down through the cloudy sky, illuminating the sparsely furnished room. This was the window someone had spied on them from the day before, she realized. The burst of white—it had been this woman's sari. From deep within the armoire, the elderly woman pulled out a cloth-wrapped bundle and laid it on her narrow bed. With agile fingers she pulled aside the cotton sheet, and inside sat a scuffed and dented metal chest. On it was engraved *RMT*.

Epilogue

Wednesday, September 21
New Delhi, India

Mrs. Hackworth, I need to be totally honest with you. As you've probably figured out by now, my trip to India didn't go exactly as Zara and I thought it would. But during my crazy dash to my grandmother's house, I met some wonderful, kindhearted people. And some who were far from nice. Okay, they were dirty crooks who would probably sell their mother for a nickel. But like Pakistan, India is a land of contradictions.

There is extreme poverty and wealth, charity and greed, beauty and ugliness, prejudice and tolerance. Throughout the journey, I looked for the part of me that was Indian. And you know what? It was always there, coexisting with all the Pakistani parts, like kebab and paratha, the perfect combination.

Going back to what happened at my grandmother's old house. I don't remember much after I saw my great-grandfather's initials on the chest. It's all pretty much a blur in my tired brain. I remember my mother, Syeda Khala, and Zara showing up at the house, then people shouting, laughing, crying, and hugging, all at the same time. When everyone calmed down, we sat on the veranda and the woman in the white sari told us her story.

Her name is Reshma Tripathi, which sent a spark of recognition through me. This was the Reshma . . . Naniamma's best friend! She looked so sad as she told us what had happened the day her father dropped my grandmother and her family off at the train station. When he'd returned home, he'd told them that

Dr. Tauheed wanted him to take care of his house, and that the family would return if life in Pakistan didn't suit them. They had waited years for a letter or phone call. But none had come. She said her father had died wondering what had happened to his friend. When they heard the terrible stories about those crossing Partition lines, they feared the worst.

Of course it was my sister who asked her what she was doing in Naniamma's house, which got her the stink—eye from Mom for being rude. But I'm glad she asked. I was dying to know too. Reshma wasn't offended, though. She said that when the Indian government started confiscating abandoned Muslim properties, her father had taken ownership of the house. It was empty till he gave it to Reshma when she got married. She lived there with her husband and son. Finally, I asked her how she found the chest. It was a monsoon storm, back in 1972, the year her husband died, that had caused a tree in the garden to topple over. The gardener found the chest while digging out the tree.

When she saw the initials scratched into its side, Reshma knew immediately who it belonged to, and she had kept it safe ever since.

Maya tucked the pink pencil into the journal's pages and leaned back in the lumpy chair. Every bruised limb scrubbed clean, wearing fresh clothes, sore feet tucked up under a soft shawl, she sighed. Somehow she'd made it through the entire journey without doing serious damage to herself, though she'd come precariously close multiple times. And once her mom had finished hugging her to death, she'd informed Maya that she and Zara were going to be seriously grounded when they got home. *But,* she thought, *it was all worth it.* She gazed out over the hospital room, where *Naniamma* reclined against pillows, sipping a steaming cup of tea, nibbling biscuits. Tucked up beside her sat Reshma, giggling, both their eyes radiant as Maya's mom and aunts fretted over the chest, trying to get it open.

"Isn't it amazing?" said Zara, coming up from behind, carrying a third plate of kebabs and *parathas* for Maya.

The sisters' gaze met and without having to say it, they knew exactly what the other meant. It was beyond awesome how everything had worked out.

"You did it, you know," continued Zara, admiration settling over her delicate features.

"No," said Maya, taking the plate. "It was all your idea. You got us to India, then convinced me that we should look for the chest."

"But you're the one who found it," said Zara. "It was dangerous and nutso crazy, but somehow you got to *Naniamma*'s house and got Mom to follow you."

"Okay, okay." Maya smiled. "You're right about that part." Zara grinned and ruffled Maya's hair. "You're not the quiet little mouse anymore, are you," she said. It was more of a statement than a question.

Maya narrowed her eyes and smiled. "And you're not quite the bullheaded rhino."

Before Maya could reach for another kebab, despite her full stomach, an excited voice called out from the bed.

"Girls, come here," said *Naniamma*.

Dutifully, the sisters hurried over just as their mom managed to pry open the ancient, rusty lock on the chest. Everyone in the room stared as Syeda *Khala* gently lifted the lid. Inside the squat metal box lay a protective layer of fabric coated with a thick layer of dust.

"Take it out," whispered *Naniamma*, two spots of color on her pale cheeks.

Syeda *Khala* lifted what looked to be an old linen tablecloth, protecting the contents underneath.

A book lay on top, which Dalia lifted with trembling fingers. "It's a Quran," she murmured, opening the cover.

Syeda *Khala* leaned over her shoulder to inspect the yellow pages. "It's our family tree," she whispered in wonder.

The sisters stared at the list of names, written out in elegant Urdu script—great-grandparents, uncles, aunts, and cousins, long gone and nearly forgotten, as if they had never existed at all. *They were real people,* thought Maya, *and they are a part of me. And they live on through us.*

Sofia *Khala* lifted a stack of frayed documents, set it aside, and then removed a disintegrating cardboard box.

"Give that to me," said *Naniamma*, reaching for it eagerly. A whiff of mothballs escaped as she tugged it open. Underneath sat a stack of black-and-white photos. With shaking fingers she raised the one on top. A lithe, graceful woman in an embroidered silk sari posed in a photographer's studio, four little girls in frilly dresses beside her staring into the lens. The one in the middle stood out. In her rounded features Maya could see *Naniamma*'s face. Hands on her hips, a stubborn tilt to her jaw, the girl had a naughty grin across her face. That stubbornness, Maya realized, was a trait she'd inherited as well, like peas in a pod. *Naniamma* gazed down at her mother's face, tears glistening along her lashes. Maya sucked in a breath at the sight of her grandmother seeing her mother's face for the first time in over half a century. *Naniamma* glanced up, and her eyes met Maya's. The joy Maya saw there made her heart swell. Zara gently lifted out another picture, a shot of the entire family sitting in the garden. In their faces Maya saw herself.

Sofia *Khala* had removed a large leather box from the bottom of the chest. "This is heavy," she exclaimed, unlatching its tarnished silver buckles.

Secreted inside were frayed velvet pouches filled with a collection of family jewels—gold bangles studded with emeralds, necklaces strung with rubies and uncut diamonds, matching earrings, and traditional anklets of heavy silver—all handed down through the generations.

But it was a small tin box that caught *Naniamma*'s eye. Biting her lip, she opened the lid, revealing four topaz rings, large enough to fit a man's finger. "Give me your hand, *jaan*," she said, staring intently at Maya.

Maya held up her hand and her grandmother placed the ring at its center. The cool, heavy metal nestled in her palm.

"*Nanabba* promised to bring you back to India one day," whispered Maya, chest tightening. He would have been thrilled that they found the chest. For him the journey alone, with his beloved wife, would have been enough.

"And because of you, his promise was fulfilled," said *Naniamma*, reaching out to cup her chin. "And he will have his ring—all because of you."

Sharing a teary look with Zara, Maya handed the ring back to her grandmother, who slipped it onto her thumb. *Naniamma* then reached for the gold bangles, inlaid with emeralds. The round stones reminded Maya of peas, a vegetable she'd grown fond of these past few days. The gems' dark green represented good luck and renewal, she knew. Gently, her grandmother slipped one on each girl's arm. "These were my mother's. Whenever you look at them, remember that you are connected to her and our family," she said.

The girls nodded and settled onto a corner of the bed. Maya glanced back with a shiver. In all the hubbub, she had momentarily forgotten something critical. Lying on a mat on the floor, passed out after eating enough to stuff a baby elephant, slumbered two small figures, cocooned in a soft coverlet. Jai's arm lay draped over Guddi peacefully. Maya smiled, recalling the moment the siblings had seen each other. True to her word, Maya had convinced her mother that the first thing they needed to do was to return to Agra and find Guddi. On the way they had called Sofia *Khala*, who was at the hospital with *Naniamma*. It turned out that *Naniamma*'s doctor, Dr. Kumar, was on the board of Railway Children, a charity that rescued orphaned and abandoned children. After collecting information from Maya and Jai, she'd placed a few critical phone calls, leading to a raid at the warehouse. Although they were still on the lookout for Boss and the boys, Mini and the other children had been rescued and placed in orphanages, where they were being well looked after.

Maya's mother and aunts, after a long conversation, had decided to enroll Jai and Guddi in a respected boarding school. Reshma would be keeping an eye on them. Maya hoped to keep in touch with them and see them again soon. Maya sat at the foot of the bed, surrounded by women she loved, thinking what an amazing story it all was. *Good enough to make a Bolly-*

wood movie out of it, she thought, smiling inwardly. Somehow, she had lived up to all the meanings of the name Maya—the bearing of a princess, depth of an eternal spring, and love, coupled with the gumption and strength of the mothers of Hermes and Buddha and the invincible power of Durga.

> *. . . Ishwar Allah tere naam*
> *Sab ko sanmati de Bhagwan. . . .*

> *(Ishwar [Hindu name for God] and Allah*
> *[Muslim name for God] are but names for You.*
> *Oh, God, grant us some wisdom.)*

—Hymn sung by Gandhi and his followers

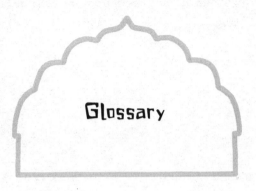

Glossary

abbu: "Father" in Urdu

akoori: Spicy Indian scrambled eggs

Allah: Standard Arabic word for God, used by Muslims as well as Arab Christians

Ameen: or *Amen*. Celebration marking the end of a child's reading of the Quran

ammi: "Mother" in Urdu

baji: "Older sister" in Urdu and Hindi

bhabi: "Sister-in-law" in Urdu and Hindi

bindi: Forehead decoration worn in South Asia, traditionally a red dot, and said to be the sixth *chakra*, the seat of "concealed wisdom," and protection against demons or bad luck

bodhi: Enlightenment possessed by a Buddha regarding the nature of things

chaiwallah: Tea seller

chowkidar: Caretaker and watchman

daal: Stew made out of lentils, spices, and sometimes vegetables

dhaba: Roadside restaurant usually at a truck stop

Durga: Hindu goddess of the universe, believed to be the power behind the work of creation, preservation, and destruction of the world

gulab: "Rose" in Urdu

gulabi: The color pink in Urdu and Hindi

Gulabi Gang: Group of Indian women vigilantes and activists founded by Sampat Pal Devi to stop injustice against women

halwa: Indian dessert consisting of carrots or semolina boiled with milk, almonds, sugar, butter, and cardamom

Hindi: Language spoken throughout most of northern India

Hindu: Follower of Hinduism, a major religion of India

imam: Holy man who leads Islamic worship services, serves as a community leader, and provides religious guidance

jaan: "Darling" or "dearest" in Urdu

jhuggi: Shantytown

kebab: Spicy grilled meats

kameez: Long, flowing shirt

khala: "Aunt" in Urdu

kurta pyjama: Long shirt and loose pants; common outfit in India and Pakistan

Muslim: Adherent of Islam, a monotheistic Abrahamic religion based on the Quran

namaste: Customary Hindu greeting when individuals meet or part

nanabba: "Maternal grandfather" in Urdu

naniamma: "Maternal grandmother" in Urdu

Navaratri: Also known as Durga Puja; Hindu festival of nine nights dedicated to the glorification of Shakti, the feminine form of the divine

paratha: Layered flatbread

puri: Round, unleavened wheat bread of India, usually deep fried

Quran: Central religious text of Islam, which Muslims believe to be a revelation from God

roti: Whole wheat flatbread resembling a tortilla

Sahib: Form of address or title placed after a man's name or designation, used as a mark of respect

Salaam Alaikum: Arabic spoken greeting used by Muslims as well as Arabs; means "Peace be upon you"

shalwar kameez: Baggy pants and long shirt worn by both men and women in India and Pakistan

Sikh: Follower of Sikhism, a monotheistic religion that originated in the fifteenth century in the Punjab region

tatti: Hindi, Urdu, and Punjabi word for poo

tehzeeb: "Culture and manners" in Urdu

Urdu: South Asian language in the Indo-Aryan branch of the Indo-European family of languages; national language of Pakistan, official language of five Indian states, and one of the twenty-two scheduled languages in the Constitution of India

vindaloo: Highly spiced, hot Indian curry from the Goan Coast

Walaikum Salaam: Traditional response to "Salaam Alaikum"; means "And upon you be peace"

Acknowledgments

A BOOK COMES INTO the world with the help of many hands. Thanks to my agent, Michael Bourret, who has gently guided my writing career. Much admiration to the extraordinary team at Simon & Schuster who take my words and turn them into books! My publisher, Paula Wiseman, who continues to believe in my work. And Sylvie Frank—part editor, part counselor, and part lion tamer—who wrung every last bit from me to create the best book possible. I was inspired by scholars and writers who've spent their lives examining the history and culture of the Indian subcontinent, in particular my professors at UC Berkeley and Columbia University—Bruce Pray, Ayesha Jalal, and Frances Pritchett. And historians Yasmin Khan and William Dalrymple, and innumerable writers whose stories I grew up reading. Thank you to family and friends who've provided their personal accounts of Partition and the impact it had on their lives. To my first line of readers, Hena Khan, Imtiaz Ghori, Farah Hasnat, and Michelle Chew—you are awesome. And of course to my two beloved peanuts—Farid and Zakaria Senzai.

Author's note

AFTER WRITING TWO BOOKS based largely on my husband's family stories from Afghanistan, I decided to delve into my own family's history, rooted in India. As I dug deeper into my past, I kept coming back to August 14, 1947, and the Great Partition that divided Pakistan from India. Both my parents and their families were born in India, yet they (like millions of other Muslim families) had to decide whether to stay in their ancestral homeland, India, or to emigrate to Pakistan, a country established for Muslims. In the end, my *dadiamma* (father's mother) refused to budge from our estate in Northern India. Like her, half of India's Muslims chose to stay put. My *naniamma* (mother's mother) and her family, like Alia's parents, decided to move to Pakistan. My grandfather left a thriving medical practice and much of what they owned behind, and made the perilous journey to Pakistan. As Muslims streamed out of India, Hindus and Sikhs left Pakistan, leading to the single largest migration of people in history. Towns, villages, and entire cities were uprooted, as unparalleled violence erupted across the coutry.

That history has shaped who I am and continues to

be a strong part of my identity. When people ask me, "Are you from India or Pakistan?" I don't have a simple answer. My paternal grandparents are buried in India, while my maternal grandparents are buried in Pakistan. I have deep roots in both countries and continue to visit both. Since I was born in the United States, I cannot claim citizenship to either. In the end, I explain that I'm from both. It is a response shared by millions of others who faced a similar fate. Throughout history, India was a mosaic of identities, divided along various ethnic, racial, religious, and linguistic lines. There was conflict between them, but they had co-existed, blending culture, arts, architecture, literature, and cuisine. But after a century of British rule, deep fissures had formed. And as independence loomed, rival groups jockeyed for power. One of the clearest lines of demarcation fell along religious tensions, as clashes between calculating Jawaharlal Nehru, idealistic Mahatma Gandhi, and taciturn Muhammad Ali Jinnah came to head.

Seventy years later, India and Pakistan, both nuclear powers, have fought two wars against each other and continue to employ campaigns of subterfuge and terror across their borders—struggling as only true siblings can. Neither country's fate has been ideal, but

India is economically better off and politically more stable, while Pakistan has struggled with military coups and economic hardship since Jinnah's death, just thirteen months after Partition.

As a product of both countries, I find it disheartening to watch Indian and Pakistani politicians continue to promulgate antipathy and vitriol towards one another. Recently elected Hindu hardliners such as Modi in India and religious extremists in Pakistan continue to play the nationalist card and invoke hatred along religious lines. This is especially disheartening since both countries have also failed to address key issues at home: poverty; women and children's rights; access to education; and the rights of class, caste, and minorities.

Both countries have paid a heavy price for Partition and there are many on both sides who question whether Partition should have occurred. Even in my family there are those who feel it was beneficial and those who vehemently insist it was a terrible mistake. It was after talking with both ends of the spectrum that *Ticket to India* came to life. The story is mostly fiction, but it also provides a glimpse into historic events that impacted millions. The reason I felt so compelled to tell this story is that so few kids in the

West have heard of Partition. While kids may know something about Gandhi, spicy curries, yoga, or the Taj Mahal, few know about the history of these two countries. While my aim was to share this difficult and painful story, it was also an opportunity to shed light on the rich culture, diversity, and history of the Indian subcontinent.

—N. H. S.